Heartland™
Holding Fast

Eloise strode more confidently towards her horse. Molly threw up her head and backed off. Eloise stopped. "I can't," she called, biting her lip. "How can it be right to drive her away? She might not come back."

"She will," Amy promised. She jumped down from the fence and went to stand beside Eloise. But as she got closer, she realized to her alarm that the young woman was close to tears.

"She'll come back to you. She won't to me," said Eloise in a trembling voice. "I can't send her away. I really can't."

Read all the books about Heartland:

Coming Home
After the Storm
Breaking Free
Taking Chances
Come What May
One Day You'll Know
Out of the Darkness
Thicker Than Water
Every New Day
Tomorrow's Promise
True Enough
Sooner or Later
Darkest Hour
Everything Changes
Love is a Gift
Holding Fast
A Season of Hope
Winter Memories (Special Edition)
New Beginnings
From This Day On
Always There

www.scholastic.co.uk/zone

Heartland™

Holding Fast

Lauren Brooke

With special thanks to Gill Harvey

Scholastic Children's Books,
Euston House, 24 Eversholt Street,
London NW1 1DB, UK
a division of Scholastic Ltd

London ~ New York ~ Toronto ~ Sydney ~ Auckland
Mexico City ~ New Delhi ~ Hong Kong

First published in the UK by Scholastic Ltd, 2004
Series created by Working Partners Ltd

Copyright © Working Partners Ltd, 2004

Heartland is a trademark of Working Partners Ltd

10 digit ISBN 0 439 96869 9
13 digit ISBN 978 0439 96869 0

All rights reserved

Printed and bound by Nørhaven Paperback A/S, Denmark

4 6 8 10 9 7 5

Chapter One

"I can see them! They're over there!" Amy said excitedly, pointing along the row of expectant faces at the arrivals gate of the airport.

"Where?" asked Amy's sister Lou, craning her neck. Amy pointed again to where two broad-shouldered figures stood, wearing jeans and plaid shirts, waiting with big smiles at the far end of the barrier. Lou beckoned to her boyfriend Scott while Amy grinned and waved, then pushed her trolley a little faster.

"Ty! Grandpa!" Amy reached Ty and let go of her trolley to fling her arms around him. He laughed into her hair and held her tight.

"Oh, it's so good to see you!" Amy exclaimed, letting go of Ty to give Jack a big hug, too. "I've really missed you!"

"Not as much as we've missed you," said Ty. "We're really glad that Australia let us have you back."

"Of course it did," said Amy, as Lou and Scott came up to join in with the round of welcoming hugs. "You didn't think I'd want to stay with Dad, did you?"

Ty looked down at her, his soft green eyes smiling. "It crossed my mind. But only for – oh, about two and a half seconds."

Amy laughed and hugged him again. There had never been any doubt in her own mind, not even for an instant. This was where she wanted to be – back in Virginia with Ty and

Grandpa, heading home to Heartland and the horses that she worked with. It had been fantastic to see her father Tim's beautiful stables, to meet his wife Helena and their baby daughter Lily, but it had made Amy realize that Heartland was where she belonged.

"The car's in the parking lot," said Jack, picking up Amy's bag. "Let's get going. You must be exhausted."

Lou nodded. "You could say that," she agreed. "It was some flight. Even with Scott's shoulder for a pillow, I didn't get any sleep."

They all crowded into Jack Bartlett's station wagon with their luggage, and set off. Amy was squashed in next to Ty in the front seat, and she reached for his hand to give it a squeeze. She was tired and jet-lagged from the long journey, but her happiness at seeing him had given her a burst of energy.

"I'm dying to hear about everything that's been happening," she said. "You haven't been overdoing it, have you?"

"I'm fine," Ty assured her. "I've just been doing as much work as I can, and stopping when it gets too much. I'm feeling better, honestly."

Amy looked at Ty's face and believed him. It seemed incredible that only a few months ago he had been lying in a coma, critically ill after a tornado had destroyed the horse barn while he was inside, and Amy had wondered if he would ever come back to her. But here he was, looking tanned from his outdoor life again, chatting about life at Heartland.

"How's Dazzle?" Amy asked.

Dazzle was a mustang stallion who had come to Heartland while Ty was still in a coma. It hadn't been easy for Amy to connect with him, but the horse had developed a special bond with Ty when he had come out of hospital.

Ty smiled. "He's doing great," he said. "It won't be long before he's ready to go back to his owners."

That was the way things worked at Heartland — horses came to be gentled or to be treated for problems, but they always had to leave again to make room for others. Amy knew it would be tough for Ty to see Dazzle go.

She squeezed his hand. "At least I'm back," she whispered.

As they bumped their way up the familiar Heartland driveway, Amy felt as though she'd been away for months rather than just a few weeks. Despite her tiredness, she couldn't wait to see all the horses. But when they turned into the stable yard, she could see that there was no chance of that — not immediately, at least.

A crowd of people stood outside the farmhouse, waving and cheering as the station wagon came to a halt. There was Ben, the other stablehand; Amy's schoolfriend Soraya with her boyfriend Matt, Scott's brother; Ty's mom was standing there too, next to Grandpa's friend, Nancy... Amy stared at them in disbelief. They hadn't been away that long!

Amy and Lou jumped out and everyone quickly gathered around. After a big round of hugs and kisses, Nancy clapped her hands to get everyone's attention. She was wearing an apron over her neat blue jeans and shirt, and Amy guessed she'd been cooking. Her heart sank at the idea of a big sit-down meal. She felt too tired to eat and she just wanted to visit the horses before having a shower and a nap. She glanced sideways at Lou, but her sister was talking to Scott and his brother, and didn't notice the look on Amy's face.

"Supper's ready," Nancy announced. "You must be starving after that long flight. Come on in."

Amy looked longingly at the stables. After being stuck on a crowded plane for twenty hours, she craved the peace of the yard. All this fuss – she just wasn't in the mood for it. But Ty put his arm around her, and Amy let him steer her inside to sit down at the kitchen table.

Nancy had been busy. A huge roast chicken sat waiting to be carved, surrounded by crispy roast potatoes. A steaming gravy boat sat next to it, and a big platter of fresh green beans and peas. Nancy looked flushed and happy, her blue eyes sparkling as she handed the carving knife to Grandpa and started dishing out the vegetables.

Amy felt a wave of exhaustion wash over her. The smiling faces around the table seemed as though they were far away, chatting in distant voices. A plate of food was placed in front of her, so she picked up her knife and fork and mechanically began to chew a piece of chicken. She could tell it was beautifully cooked, but it was the last thing she wanted right now. She made a huge effort and kept on eating while everyone laughed at Lou's description of little Lily.

"Ow – that was her name for me," she said. "She couldn't say the 'l'. And she called Amy, 'Amee'. She's a real cutie, isn't she, Amy?"

"Sorry?" said Amy, coming out of her reverie. "Oh — Lily. Yes, she's lovely."

She gave Lou a small smile. The truth was that it had taken her a while to get used to her baby half-sister. For one thing, she was more used to dealing with horses than little humans; and accepting her father's second family hadn't been easy, either. She listened as Lou talked about Helen and Tim, and her trip with Scott to Ayers Rock.

As Lou described the amazing red desert landscape, Amy saw her exchange glances with Scott. "We've got something to announce," said Lou, smiling across the table at the tanned vet. "Scott proposed on the top of the rock. And I said yes. We're engaged!"

Jack got to his feet, beaming. "Well, that's wonderful," he said, raising his glass. "I must admit that we had an inkling — hence the welcome-home party — but it's great to hear for sure. Congratulations! I think we should have a toast. Let's raise our glasses to Lou and Scott!"

"Lou and Scott!" chorused everyone, with a lively chink of glasses.

"I spotted Scott in a jeweller's a few weeks back," Nancy confessed, when the hubbub had died down. "I guessed he'd propose in Australia, so I took a chance and got everyone together. Now, when's the big day? Have you decided yet?"

Lou looked slightly taken aback. "Oh, we haven't sorted out any specifics yet," she said. "It's a bit early for that."

Matt thumped his brother on the shoulder. "Great stuff, Scott," he said. "You'll have to watch out for Mom, though. She'll have a field day organizing everything. "

"Traditionally, it's the bride's side of the family that does the organizing," Nancy told him. "Your mother won't have anything to worry about."

"I'm sure she will anyway," grinned Matt. "She won't let a little detail like not having any daughters stop her pitching in!"

"Well, it can make things quite difficult when both sides of the couple get involved," said Nancy cautiously. "But I'm sure it will all work out beautifully, if you allow enough time for planning. That's why it's good to set a date nice and early. Isn't that right, Jack?"

Grandpa nodded. Amy thought he looked happier than she'd ever seen him, sitting with Nancy on one side and Lou on the other. "The sooner the better. Why not?" he said.

But as the conversation bounced around the table, Lou began to look a little uneasy. "Really, we're not making any definite plans yet," she insisted. "There's far too much to deal with at Heartland first."

Amy stared at her sister, the words slowly sinking in. When Lou had told her in Australia that she and Scott were getting engaged, she hadn't really thought what it might mean. For some reason, she had assumed that it wouldn't make much difference to their everyday lives. But now it dawned on her, for the first time, that Lou would be leaving Heartland...

* * *

The main course was over at last, and Amy felt relieved as Nancy took her plate away. Perhaps she could just slip out for some fresh air and see the horses.

"I'm just popping outside," she said in a low voice to Ty.

Amy got up and headed for the door. It would be so lovely to see Sundance, Sugarfoot the little Shetland, Jasmine, all the Heartland residents as well as the new arrivals. She was walking across the yard in the quiet night air when a voice stopped her. It was Lou.

"Amy! Are you OK?"

Amy smiled wanly. "I'm fine. Just tired. I wanted to see the horses..."

Lou nodded. "I know." She took a deep breath. "It's all a bit much. I didn't expect there to be so much fuss about our engagement. You're not upset, are you?"

"Upset? Why should I be upset?" Amy asked carefully.

"Well ... because it'll change everything, I guess."

Amy was silent. She couldn't lie to Lou – her sister knew her too well for that – but at the same time she didn't want to spoil her excitement. "It won't be really soon, though, will it?" she said eventually.

"No," said Lou. "We don't want to fix a date yet, whatever everyone's saying. All this talk about the wedding – it's like Scott and I are suddenly the guests of honour or something. It's all a bit much. I feel so jet-lagged. I just want some sleep..."

"I know what you mean," said Amy, feeling fatigue seeping through her.

Lou sighed. "I'd better go back in. Nancy's serving up

dessert." She looked at Amy, a slight plea in her eyes. "You'll come back in, right?"

Amy looked around the yard and realized that the horses would have to wait. She didn't want to leave Lou to deal with all the attention on her own. She took Lou's arm, and they went back inside.

Amy sat back down next to Ty. He threw her a questioning glance and she squeezed his hand reassuringly. Nancy was cutting into an enormous home-made blueberry cheesecake, and despite her tiredness, Amy couldn't resist it. She gave the older woman a warm smile. Nancy sure could cook.

The party atmosphere calmed down a little as everyone tucked into dessert. Soraya and Matt told everyone about the weekend they had spent with Soraya's aunt and uncle in a cabin in the woods while Amy had been away. It sounded like fun and they were obviously getting along really well as a couple. Amy sighed. She'd be back to school in a couple of days and she wondered if Matt and Soraya would want her hanging around with them now that they were so close.

"I'll take you to see Dazzle after dinner if you're not too tired," Ty offered, breaking in on her thoughts.

"That would be great," Amy responded, smiling at him. "I'd love to see all the other horses, too."

At last the meal was over and Amy offered to help clear up.

Nancy wouldn't hear of it. "You need to unwind and rest," she said briskly, wiping her hands on her apron. "Go on, off you go. I can manage."

Feeling relieved, Amy slipped out and joined Ty, who was

fetching a flashlight from the tack room.

"Dazzle's still down in the bottom paddock," he explained, and they set off down through the front yard and past the newly repaired barn. The beams in the barn roof had collapsed on top of Ty during a storm, giving him the head injuries that had put him in a coma. Now that the repairs had been done, it was almost as though the nightmare had never happened... But only almost. The memories of that terrifying night would never completely be erased; and as they went down to the paddocks, Amy was aware of Ty limping a little beside her – so much better than he had been, but still not completely healed.

"How's the physio going?" she asked.

"It's hard work," Ty admitted. "But the more I work at it, the quicker I seem to improve. I'll be as good as new before long. Promise."

Ty trained the flashlight over the fence as they approached the bottom paddock. A handsome blue roan stallion loomed out of the shadows towards them, his nostrils flaring clouds of steam in the cold air.

"Hey, boy," Ty called softly. "Come and say hi to Amy."

Dazzle snorted in welcome and thrust his head over the fence. Ty fished in his pocket for some pony nuts and held them out on the palm of his hand. Dazzle stretched out his neck and delicately lipped up the nuts, blowing gently over Ty's hand. Amy's heart warmed as she reached out to scratch his neck. This Dazzle was so different from the wild, desperate creature that had arrived at Heartland, almost straight from the deserts of Nevada, furious at being deprived of his freedom. Amy couldn't help feeling that the desert was where he truly belonged; but given that there wasn't a choice for him, she knew the stallion would be fine now that he had learned to respect and enjoy human company.

Dazzle nudged Ty, hoping for more nuts, and Ty laughed. "He knows I'm a soft touch," he said.

He fed the stallion another handful, then he and Amy walked back up to the yard. They did a round of the barn, saying hello to all the horses before finishing up in the front yard.

"Come and meet Molly," said Ty. "She's only been here a couple of days. I've been letting her settle in."

He stopped at the first stall and Amy peered past him. A sleek-limbed, bright bay mare was dozing at the back of the stall, resting one hind leg. She woke as Ty switched the light on, and turned her head to give a deep whicker of welcome. Amy took in her slightly dished face and big, gentle eyes. She was a beauty.

"She's lovely," said Amy. "And she seems so friendly. What's her history?"

"She's part quarter-horse, part Arab," said Ty. "Owned by a woman called Eloise Beatson. She's about Lou's age and she mostly uses Molly for trail riding."

"So what's the problem?" asked Amy. "She looks like she'd be a great ride."

"Yeah," agreed Ty. "But she's been difficult recently. Eloise says she was riding her through a creek a month or so ago and she stepped on a sharp stone that cut through her frog. The cut developed into an abscess, which was treated with antibiotics. But when Eloise started riding her again, Molly wasn't the same. She'll spook at anything now, even things like long grass or shadows. It seems like she's completely lost her nerve."

"Poor girl," murmured Amy.

She let herself into the stall and ran her hand lightly over the bay's shoulder. Molly looked around, flicking one of her ears back. Amy studied her. The lines of her body were relaxed, and trust shone out of her large, dark eyes. There were no signs at all of bad temper or a difficult nature.

"She doesn't look like the type to bear a grudge," she commented.

"That's what I thought," Ty agreed. "She's sensitive, but there's nothing mean about her."

Amy worked her fingers in little circles up Molly's neck, and felt the mare relax almost immediately. She was clearly a horse that enjoyed connecting with humans and responded well to attention. "What was it like when Eloise left her?"

"She was pretty upset. She called after her for about half an hour," said Ty. "We gave her some Rescue Remedy, and Ben stayed in the stable with her. She calmed down after a while, but she's a loyal one. There's no doubting the bond between her and Eloise."

Amy smiled. She'd missed this so much in recent months — being with Ty and discussing the horses with him, knowing that they understood each other. First there had been Ty's coma, then her trip to Australia. But now they were both back, and life could return to normal — at last.

Chapter Two

The chestnut gelding and his rider seemed to fly around the jumps in the training ring. The jumps were over a metre high, but the horse's ears were pricked forward and, with his rider's help, he judged each one perfectly.

Amy applauded as the pair cleared the final fence and slowed to a controlled canter, then a trot.

"Bravo, Ben!" she called. "You and Red are looking fantastic."

Ben rode over, clapping Red on the neck as he did so.

"Thanks, Amy," he said. "Things are going well, actually. We stand a really good chance at Brideswell next Saturday."

It was Tuesday evening, and Amy had been back at school for two days. It was a shock to the system after her vacation, but at least she'd managed to keep up with all her assignments while she was away. Even so, she'd been especially glad to escape school that afternoon – her French class had seemed to drag on for ever.

She smiled up at Ben. "Well, I hope you bring home the blue ribbon," she said.

"We will if I keep Red on form," said Ben. "Actually, I was hoping to take a couple of days off next week before the show, to make sure he peaks at the right time."

Amy frowned. She wasn't sure that they could spare Ben so easily while she was at school, especially as Ty was still having physio – though she knew he fully deserved a break after all the work he'd put in. "I'll need to check with Ty," she said. "He might not be able to cover—"

To her surprise, Ben interrupted her. "Oh, forget it," he said. "I should have known Heartland would have to come first."

Abruptly, he turned Red and rode off down the training ring at a brisk trot.

Amy's mouth dropped open. She watched Ben ride away and wondered whether to call him back; but he was already working at winding down with Red, taking him over some smaller jumps to finish the session. Amy turned and went back up to the yard, feeling slightly hurt and bewildered.

She knew Ben had had his own share of difficult times recently. Red had contracted the flu and hadn't been able to compete for weeks, and with Ty in the hospital, Ben had worked really hard around the yard, even taking on some of Amy's chores so that she could concentrate on treating the horses. Then he'd missed his chance with Soraya, who had started going out with Matt. To top things off, Amy had gone to Australia, leaving Ben with a heavier workload yet again. No wonder he was feeling aggrieved. Amy decided she should arrange some days off for him as soon as possible.

As she approached the yard, Amy heard Lou calling her from the farmhouse door. She broke into a jog. "What is it?"

"There's been a call," said Lou as Amy followed her into the kitchen. "It's kind of … interesting. I wanted to talk it through with you before we say anything to anyone else."

Amy was intrigued. "Really? What kind of call?"

Lou picked up a news article from a web page that was lying on the table. "Do you remember this?" she asked, handing the paper to Amy.

Amy looked at the date at the top of the page and her heart began to pound. It was the day after the storm – the day when it had seemed that her whole world was falling apart and she had almost lost Ty. She read the headline: "Hero Police Officer Makes Dramatic Rescue". She glanced at Lou and shook her head. The last thing she'd wanted to do right after the storm was follow the news.

"Read on," said Lou.

Amy scanned the article. "'Sergeant Mark Garcia became a hero last night when he rescued three youths from an overturned car in a breaker's yard. The boys, all aged 14, were sitting in a scrapped car when the storm struck. The car was spun over by one of the series of tornadoes whipped up by the storm, trapping the boys inside. One boy's leg was broken in three places, but thanks to Sergeant Garcia's swift actions, no further injuries occurred. All three boys are now in a comfortable state in hospital, and two are expected to return home by this evening.

"'Unfortunately Sergeant Garcia's patrol horse was also injured in the course of the rescue…'"

Amy put the paper down. "What happened to the horse? Is that what the call was about?"

Lou nodded. "Apparently Venture – that's the horse – seemed to recover from his injuries, but has never been the same since. His vets are puzzled, because all the tests suggest he should be fine by now. But he still behaves as though he's in pain, and he hates being ridden, even by Sergeant Garcia. I think the police are turning to us as a last resort. If we can't do anything with him, they'll just retire him."

Amy thought for a moment. Any reminder of that night would be difficult for everyone at Heartland, but especially for Ty. "Ty might not be able to face it," she said slowly. "I'd need to discuss it with him first."

"Yes, of course," agreed Lou. "I can foresee a few other problems, too. The papers are still following the story, so we'd get quite a lot of media attention. That's all very well, but Venture will have received the best treatment money can buy already – police horses are valuable and they go through a long training process. We might not be able to do anything for him, which could look bad. You know how the papers twist everything."

Amy frowned. "I'm not so worried about that side of things," she said. She realized that her instinct to help a horse in pain was kicking in already, despite the obstacles. "It's Venture that counts, not what the papers say. We might be able to help."

Lou smiled. "I thought you might say that," she said.

"I'd need to check him out, though," said Amy. "If Ty feels comfortable with it, do you think you could arrange for me to visit?"

"That's a good idea," said Lou. "Let me know what he thinks. I said I'd call them back tomorrow." She looked around as Jack came through the door with Nancy. "Hi there," she greeted them.

"Hello, Lou," said Nancy, kissing her on the cheek. "And you, Amy."

Amy smiled and offered her cheek for Nancy to kiss. Jack took off his coat and held out his hand for Nancy's.

"Oh, thank you, Jack," said Nancy. She shrugged it off and handed it to him, then pulled a big plastic sealed container out of her bag. "I know how busy you all are," she said. "So I cooked a casserole for us all to have for supper. It just needs heating up."

Lou looked taken aback. "Oh," she said. "You didn't need to do that, Nancy. I've already made a pie. That just needs heating up, too."

There was an edge to her voice, and Amy looked at her in surprise.

"Oh, I am sorry, Lou," said Nancy. "I just assumed…"

"Assumed what?" queried Lou, raising her eyebrows.

Nancy flushed and glanced quickly at Grandpa.

"Two dinners! We are doing well," said Jack Bartlett, with a chuckle. "Perhaps we could have the pie tomorrow, Lou. That'll save you some time, won't it?"

Lou pursed her lips, then forced them into a smile. "I guess so," she said, and took the container from Nancy. "Thanks, Nancy." She tipped the casserole into a saucepan and put it on low heat on the stove. "Could you stir that for me, Amy?" she asked. "I'm just going upstairs to change."

Lou left the kitchen. Amy watched her go, feeling baffled. It wasn't like Lou to take offence over such a little thing – and besides, it was obvious that Nancy was only trying to help.

She stirred the casserole with a wooden spoon, sniffing it appreciatively. It smelt delicious.

After a while Lou came back downstairs and helped Amy dish up dinner. She was quieter than usual, but otherwise she seemed fine. Amy decided it was probably best to let it go. Lou was as busy as the rest of them, settling back into the Heartland routine after their trip. It was hardly surprising if she was a bit tense.

The next morning, Amy got up early to work with the horses before school, as usual. It hadn't taken her long to get back into her routine – almost as though she'd never been away. She dressed quickly and went down to the front yard. Molly had her head over her stall door, and whinnied a welcome when she saw Amy.

Amy smiled. Molly sure was an affectionate horse.

"Hi there, girl," she greeted her. "You're up bright and early!"

She unbolted the stall door and slipped a halter over her head. Over the last couple of days, she had been getting to know the mare by spending time in her stall, grooming her and giving her T-touch. This had reaffirmed her first impressions. Molly was responsive and friendly, and seemed to take a pleasure in people's company. Although she hadn't ridden her yet, Amy suspected that Molly's problem lay in some kind of breakdown in the relationship with her owner, and to get to the root of it she needed to establish a strong bond of trust with the mare herself.

17

She led her down to the smaller training ring and unclipped her halter. Molly remained close to her, nosing her jacket. *OK, girl, no more Mrs Nice Guy,* Amy thought to herself with a grin. She drew herself up tall, assuming an aggressive stance, and shooed her away. Molly threw up her head and ambled across the ring, but soon stopped and looked back at Amy. *Do you really want me to go away?* she seemed to say.

Amy smiled. Join-up involved driving a horse away until she chose human company of her own free will – but with Molly, there wasn't much doubt about what she wanted. She was quite happy to stay with Amy from the outset. Amy flapped her arms and ran at her anyway, knowing that a successful join-up would still be useful.

Molly snorted and trotted off around the ring. Amy drove her into a canter and kept her going for a few minutes, looking for the classic signs that the mare wanted to be with her – first flicking her ear towards Amy, then lowering her head and making chewing motions with her lips.

It didn't take long. When Amy saw that she was ready, she turned her back and waited. Soon, she soon heard Molly's soft footfalls coming across the training ring towards her, and felt her warm breath as she nuzzled her shoulder. Amy turned and patted the mare's neck, then clipped the lead rope to her halter again.

"Good girl," she murmured as Molly followed her to the gate. "That's a good start, isn't it?"

She took the mare back up to the front yard, deciding what to do next. There was little problem joining-up with Molly and working with her from the ground, but she hadn't yet tried riding her. Amy wanted to make sure that the mare trusted her completely before she did. The last thing she wanted to do was set their progress back by taking things too quickly.

As Amy let Molly back into her stall, she spotted Ben marching up from the barn, carrying empty feed buckets. He was striding along with his head down and a preoccupied expression on his face.

"Morning, Ben!" Amy called.

Ben raised his head. "Oh, hi."

He went to the yard tap and turned it on, placing the buckets under it. Amy remembered his outburst the night before. He still seemed tense.

"How's it going?" she asked, keeping her voice light. "I've finished with Molly. I can take over the feeds now, if you like."

Ben straightened up, shaking his head. "Don't worry about it. I've done the front yard. I'm just cleaning these buckets out, then I was going to do the feeds for the barn and muck out the stalls down there. I'm used to doing the lot – it won't take me long to get it over with." He hesitated, then added gruffly, "Sorry about last night. I was pretty rude."

"That's OK," said Amy. "Forget it."

She went to fetch a mucking-out fork and wheelbarrow. His words rang loud in her ears: *I'm used to doing the lot…* Amy felt a flash of guilt. Ben had seemed so willing to work hard over the last few months, but had they all taken him for granted?

She was in the middle of mucking out Jasmine's stall when she heard the sound of Mrs Baldwin's car pulling into the yard. She looked out of the stall.

"Hi there," Amy called, as Ty got out of the car and waved goodbye to his mother. He came over and gave Amy a kiss over the half-door.

"Where are you up to?" he asked. "You'll need to get ready for school soon."

"The barn stalls still need mucking out," said Amy. "But I think Ben may have started them. He's done the feeds." She paused. "Is Ben OK, by the way? Did something happen while I was away?"

Ty raised an eyebrow. "Why? What's happened?"

"He just seems a bit on edge," said Amy, and explained what Ben had said in the training ring the night before. "Then this morning, he was talking about getting the jobs over with as though he was really fed up. I feel bad. Can we spare him for a couple of days off next week, do you think?"

Ty nodded. "Yes, sure. I'll check my physio schedule and work out which days he can take. If he's feeling under pressure, I guess it would help a lot if he won at Brideswell."

"That's what I was thinking," agreed Amy. "Could you sort it out with him while I'm at school?"

"Yeah, I'll do that," said Ty.

Feeling relieved, Amy lifted another forkload of straw, then remembered her conversation with Lou the night before. "There was something else, too," she said.

Quickly, she told Ty about Venture, and the possibility of him coming to Heartland. "But there's no point in even thinking about it if it would be too difficult for you," she finished, searching Ty's face. "How would you feel if he came here?"

Ty smiled and touched her arm. "I really appreciate you asking," he said. "But I think I've been pretty lucky. I'd feel privileged to help a horse that had been injured in the same storm."

Amy smiled back. "I'm glad," she said. "I'll need to see him first anyway, and check what he's like." She picked up her fork. "I'd better get going, or I'll be late."

Amy finished the mucking out in the front yard, then dashed inside for a quick shower and flung on her school clothes before dashing downstairs again. Lou was sitting at the kitchen table going through the post with a cup of coffee in front of her.

"Ty's up for taking Venture, if the visit goes OK," Amy told her, grabbing her school bag. "So perhaps you could fix something up?"

"Sure," Lou replied. "I'll leave a message on your cellphone later."

"OK, thanks," Amy called over her shoulder, and ran down the driveway to catch the bus.

For once, the morning passed pretty quickly. Amy had geography just before lunch, which she found more interesting than a lot of her other schoolwork. They were looking at environmental issues and how America's wild spaces had shrunk over the years. She thought of Dazzle, a mustang forced

out of his natural environment, and realized that the same process was happening for millions of creatures all over the world. Perhaps Dazzle was lucky after all, she mused – at least the Bureau of Land Management ensured that he had some kind of future, even if it wasn't a wild one. Many other animals would simply die out.

When the lunchtime bell went, Amy went outside to check her cellphone. Lou had left a message. "Hi Amy, Sergeant Garcia suggests we go and see Venture this evening," said her voice. "I'll come and pick you up after school."

Amy realized she was feeling quite excited about treating this high-profile police horse, and hunted out Soraya. Her friend was in the cafeteria, lining up for the salad bar.

"Hey, guess what!" said Amy. "I'm going to the police stables tonight!"

"The police stables?" Soraya echoed.

"We might be taking one of their horses," Amy explained. "He was injured in a tornado on the same night as Ty. He never really got better and they don't know why. He's been in the papers and everything."

Soraya looked at Amy in surprise. "He was injured in the same storm?" she exclaimed. "Geez, Amy, are you going to be OK with that?"

"Why shouldn't I be?" asked Amy. "I've talked to Ty. He's fine about it, if that's what you mean."

Soraya smiled. "Sorry. I don't want to interfere or anything," she said gently. "It's just that you've been through so much already because of the storm…"

Amy nodded, her heart beating slightly faster. "I know," she admitted. "But maybe that's no bad thing. It might mean that we have something special to offer."

"You're so brave sometimes, Amy," said Soraya, squeezing her friend's arm. "I don't think I could face up to awful memories so easily. I hope it's not too painful for you."

For her? Soraya's words sank in, and Amy felt slightly disconcerted. She'd been worried for Ty, but she hadn't really thought about what she'd be facing up to herself. Now it occurred to her – the weeks of seeing Ty lying still, not knowing if he'd ever get better...

She pushed the thought away. This was different, wasn't it? There was no reason why treating a horse should remind her of that. She shook her head and smiled. "It's not me who's being brave," she said. "If Ty thinks he can handle it, I'm sure I can too."

Chapter Three

Amy was in different classes from Soraya for the rest of the day, but her friend's words stayed with her. She felt unsettled, and restless. Perhaps Soraya was right. Was it really a good idea to revisit the pain of the last few months, not knowing how it would affect everyone?

She tried to concentrate on her maths class, deciding that she would just have to wait and see. It was no good trying to guess how she'd feel until she'd met the horse and his rider for real.

At last the day was over, and Amy went to the parking lot. She spotted Lou's car and clambered in, picking up the map that Lou had placed on the dashboard.

"Where are we going?" she asked, unfolding the map.

"Venture's at a yard on the other side of town," said Lou as they turned on to the highway. "I think it's where police horses go when they retire, but it's where injuries and other problems are handled too. Sounds interesting."

Amy took a deep breath and nodded, pushing aside her anxiety. It was interesting – another yard that treated horses, but only police horses. She wondered how different their approach would be. They might not use alternative methods of treatment at all; a lot of stables didn't. It would be fascinating to find out.

A tall, broad-shouldered man with short, spiky dark hair was waiting for them at the entrance to the stables. Lou wound down her window. "Sergeant Garcia? I'm Lou Fleming, and this is Amy. We spoke on the phone."

Sergeant Garcia nodded. "Glad you could make it, Miss Fleming," he said. "You can park just round to the left, by the stable block. I'll follow you up."

Lou drove slowly to where he had indicated, giving Amy a chance to look around. The yard was large and immaculately maintained, without a trace of loose straw on the clean white concrete. She caught a glimpse of a paddock on the right where four or five horses were grazing peacefully, and also a spacious training ring. Whatever techniques they used, Amy realized that Lou was right – as far as Venture's treatment was concerned, it would have been a case of no expense spared.

Mark Garcia was standing by the stable block. There was something about his upright posture and his wide-set hazel eyes that suggested he was born to be a police officer. Amy appraised him silently. He seemed rather reserved, and it was difficult to see beyond his calm exterior. But he was welcoming enough, and as they walked around the stable block, he described what had happened on the night of the storm.

"I was on patrol out on the industrial side of town, and I'd nearly finished my shift," he explained. "The storm had blown up out of nowhere and I wanted to get Venture back to the stables. But then I heard some kids hollering from this breaker's yard."

He paused as if trying to recollect events as accurately as possible. "It turned out that the yard owner's son and some of his friends had got caught out in the storm. They'd tried to shelter in one of the old cars but a tornado whipped through the yard and turned it over."

Sergeant Garcia talked in a quiet, matter-of-fact way that belied the drama of his words. But for Amy, the description bought back the full horror of the storm. She tried to block out the memories – the crack of the barn roof and the howling wind ripping through it – but they still made her shudder, and she clenched her fists tightly. As if sensing her feelings, Lou touched her arm.

Amy threw her sister a quick, grateful smile, then turned back to the sergeant. "Go on," she said, bracing herself.

"The kids were trapped. One of them was screaming, and the car didn't look safe. I called for help, but I knew something had to be done right away. So I dismounted, and led Venture towards the car."

A frown creased his forehead. "That's when things went wrong. A gust of wind got under a pile of tyres, and a couple of them crashed down on Venture's back. He went down on his knees, then scrambled back up right away. It all happened so fast that I wasn't even sure if he'd been really injured."

They stopped outside one of the stalls and Amy read the nameplate: VENTURE. It was a relief to come back to the here and now for a moment.

"Venture! Here, boy," called Sergeant Garcia. He clicked his fingers and a beautiful dark bay horse of about seventeen hands appeared over the half-door. Amy's eyes took in his strong, stocky frame and noble head, then reached up to stroke his neck as the sergeant finished his story.

"His knees had a few cuts and he seemed shaken. I knew I shouldn't ride him until he'd been checked over, so I hooked his reins around my arm while I tried to help the kids. I managed to prise open the car door. Two of the lads scrambled out and they helped me wrench off the metal that was trapping the third. We got him out, but the poor kid was in a terrible state. It turned out he'd broken his leg in three places. I knew that moving him could have made things worse, but it was better than leaving him at further risk in that car."

"A tough decision," remarked Lou.

Mark Garcia gave a small smile. "Just part of my job," he shrugged.

Amy stroked Venture's soft nose. For all his size and strength, the horse had gentle features – a big Roman nose, large liquid eyes and a sensitive muzzle, suggesting a patient, willing character.

"What exactly were Venture's injuries?" she asked.

"The knee injuries were superficial, fortunately. His back's been more of a problem," said the sergeant. "He's seemed to be in pain ever since, but the vets can't seem to say why. He's been X-rayed and the bone structure is sound. There's a kind of stiffness about him, and he tenses up the minute anyone goes near him with a saddle – backs away and breaks into a sweat. No one can ride him." He paused, then added quietly, "Not even me."

Amy looked at him quickly. It was the first time the sergeant had given any indication of his feelings, or his attachment to

Venture. But his face was still calm, and gave nothing away. "Are you riding a different horse on duty now?" she asked.

Mark shook his head. "We tend to work with one horse at a time. I'm on ordinary station duties until Venture's ready for work again. Makes a change, but I miss riding."

Amy stared at him. *I miss riding!* she thought. *Why not say, I miss Venture?* She could feel a tide of emotion welling up. Mark Garcia's description of the storm was vivid and accurate, and yet he somehow seemed detached from it. Suddenly Amy's heart reached out to Venture, the horse who was still suffering because of that terrible night. She knew how deep the damage could go, even if his rider didn't.

"Has Venture received any alternative treatments? Any kind of massage, herbs, anything like that?" asked Lou.

The sergeant shook his head. "No. We take a very straight approach here. But one of the vets had heard of Heartland, and suggested sending Venture to you."

For an instant, a hint of awkwardness showed in his hazel eyes, and was quickly masked. But it was enough. Amy read the look in a flash. *This wasn't his idea. He doesn't believe we can help!* she realized. Determination flooded through her. She would work with Venture, and help to heal the pain that conventional methods couldn't touch.

"Can we see Venture led around the yard?" asked Lou.

"Sure," said Sergeant Garcia. "I'll just get a lead rope."

He left Amy and Lou standing by Venture's stall. Lou scratched the horse's neck. "What d'you think, Amy?" she asked. "It's kind of tricky, isn't it, when he's had all these examinations already?"

"I think we should take him," Amy burst out immediately. "They haven't tried any alternative treatments. There's so much we can do for him." She saw the surprise on Lou's face, and controlled herself. "But we'll see what he's like when he's led in hand first," she added more calmly.

The sergeant walked with long strides across the yard and let himself into Venture's stall. The powerful horse stepped carefully through the door, watching where he placed his hooves as if he was walking on a treacherous surface. Sergeant Garcia walked him slowly up the yard and back again.

Amy watched the horse from all angles. There was no obvious problem – no limp, no unevenness in his stride. But there was a definite reluctance in the way he stepped forward, as though he was nervous – but nervousness wasn't quite the right word. As Sergeant Garcia had said, there was a sort of stiffness about him, a hesitancy in his movements even when he was just walking across his own yard.

Amy was curious, and the more she watched the gelding, the more her desire to work with him grew. She looked across at Lou and caught her eye, then gave a determined little nod. Lou looked doubtful, but nodded back in agreement.

Amy stepped forward. "I think we could work with Venture at Heartland," she said. She raised her eyes to Mark's, challenging him. "If you're sure you think it's worth it," she added.

Mark looked away from her gaze. "That's great," he said. "He deserves all the help he can get."

Lou talked through the arrangements with him. They agreed that Venture should be brought over to Heartland in a couple of days' time, on Saturday. Rather apologetically, the sergeant pointed out that there was likely to be a lot of media interest and possibly even a local television crew to film Venture's arrival.

"As long as they understand that we're a stables, not a zoo," said Lou. "And that the horses must be treated with respect."

"They're used to that from coming here," the sergeant assured her. "You don't have to worry."

With everything sorted out, Amy and Lou climbed back into the car and headed back to Heartland.

"I don't think the publicity can really do any harm, do you?" asked Amy.

"Well, like I said, we'll just need to make sure they go when they're told to," said Lou. "I hope they don't come pestering us on a regular basis."

"We had to deal with them before, when we had Gallant Prince," Amy pointed out. "It wasn't too bad then."

"True," agreed Lou. "But we managed to treat him successfully, remember? That made a difference."

"Well, I think we'll treat Venture successfully, too," said Amy. "I'll make sure we do."

At school the next day, Amy decided to use her lunch hour to check out more about police horses and their training, hoping it would give her some useful insights into Venture's problems. To her astonishment, her search quickly brought up more than she had bargained for. There was a whole series of articles about Sergeant Garcia and Venture – all much more dramatic than the brief account she had seen in the newspaper. "Police Horse Crippled For Life," ran one headline. "Nothing Ventured, Nothing Gained – Police Officer Sacrifices Horse To Save Local Boys," ran another.

Amy skimmed through the articles. She was appalled at how much some of them twisted the truth. According to one account, the sergeant had ridden Venture at the car, and had managed to get the horse to kick the car door open to free the boys. It was crazy! And with a sinking feeling in her stomach, Amy suddenly realized that media attention alone wasn't the problem for Heartland. It was what they said. If reporters started over-dramatizing the work that she did, or got their facts wrong, it could do a lot of damage.

Amy took a deep breath. Venture was going to be a big challenge – but she was still certain that she had made the right decision. She thought once more of his big, noble features, and relived in her mind's eye the terrible moment when the tyres had crashed down on his back. If anyone could help a survivor of that night, it would be herself and Ty, at Heartland.

After school, Amy took Molly out for another join-up session. The late afternoon was bright and crisp, ideal for working down in the training rings. As she led the mare out, Ben crossed the yard towards her, carrying Red's tack.

"Hi, Ben," Amy greeted him. "Have you just finished training?"

Ben nodded. "Yeah. Red did really well today, so we stopped early."

"Did Ty talk to you about next week?" asked Amy, anxious to soothe the tension that still lingered between them. "It's fine for you to take some time off."

"Yes, he did, thanks," said Ben.

"That's good," said Amy. She looked at the tall, blond-haired stable hand, standing with the saddle propped on his hip, and wondered if he knew how important he was to Heartland. Ben did so much yard work and they wouldn't be able to exercise all the horses without him. But he didn't really do much on the treatment side. Why not ask him to try join-up with Molly? It was an ideal opportunity, because she was so trusting by nature.

"I'm about to join-up with Molly," she said. "D'you feel like helping me? It would be good for her."

Ben hesitated, then shook his head. "Thanks, Amy," he said. "I think I'm better off leaving all that stuff to you and Ty. And I need to clean Red's tack."

"Oh … OK," said Amy. "See you later."

As she led Molly away, she couldn't help feeling frustrated. How could anyone refuse a chance to try join-up? She wondered guiltily whether it was somehow her fault. Perhaps they should have got Ben involved with the treatment side earlier. But at least the offer had been made now. What more could she do than that?

Chapter Four

"Amy! Those are for the reporters!" exclaimed Lou, as Amy reached for a chocolate chip cookie.

Amy stepped back from the plate of cookies on the kitchen table and looked at her sister in surprise. They didn't usually make that much of a fuss for owners, let alone journalists! They were all far too busy. "I was only taking one," she protested. "They'll be too busy taking pictures to eat cookies."

It was Saturday morning. Amy had gone inside to get her gloves and found Grandpa drinking coffee in the kitchen while Lou was setting out slices of bread on the kitchen worktop.

"Some of them might have travelled quite far," said Lou. "I'm making tea and coffee, and some sandwiches for them, too."

Amy stared at her. This was definitely more fuss than usual!

"That's very generous of you, Lou," said Grandpa, taking his coffee cup to the sink. He raised an eyebrow. "Are you hoping they'll give a good report of our catering services?"

Lou flushed. "I just think we should try to give a good impression," she said. "Venture's a bigger challenge than we're used to and we don't want any bad publicity."

"I could ask Nancy to come over a bit earlier to give you a hand," Grandpa offered. "I'm sure she wouldn't mind."

"No, no, it's fine," Lou protested. She started buttering the slices of bread. "Honestly, Grandpa. It's all under control."

Amy found her gloves and made for the door. She didn't understand why Lou was in such a state. Horses arrived all the time, often in a far worse condition than Venture. As far as Amy was concerned, sandwiches for the journalists were the last thing on her mind. She needed to make sure that Venture's stall was ready.

By eleven o'clock, a handful of reporters had arrived, their cars clogging up the driveway. Grandpa soon had a parking system going, then Amy and Ty showed them around the front yard. Despite their obvious curiosity about what lay beyond, Amy refused to take them further. By the time they had finished, the local TV crew had shown up too, and the front yard seemed to be swarming with people.

Lou came out with a tray of coffee just as Nancy arrived.

"Oh Lou, let me take that," said the older woman, looking concerned. "You've got better things to be doing. If I'd known you were going to go to all this trouble, I would have come sooner to help you out."

"We can manage perfectly well," Lou responded, a little sharply. "Thanks all the same."

Amy took a mug of coffee from the tray for one of the journalists, hearing the sound of a horsebox coming up the driveway as she did so. "I think that's Venture," she said.

The horsebox rolled into the front yard, with Mark Garcia right behind in his car. He parked and jumped out to shake Amy's hand. "Good to see you again," he said. "I see the paparazzi have shown up for our local celebrity."

The sergeant seemed more relaxed away from the police stables, and Amy laughed. "Yes, but they've all been very well behaved," she said. She beckoned to Ty. "Mark, this is Ty Baldwin. He'll be working with Venture, too."

The sergeant smiled and shook Ty's hand. "I bet you'd like to get rid of all these journalists as soon as possible," he said understandingly. "Should we unload Venture right away and let them get their pictures?"

Ty helped Mark undo the bolts on the box, then allowed him to lead out the horse alone. Amy's heart went out to the gelding – despite his rigorous training, he was clearly nervous, and he flinched at the barrage of flashes that greeted him at the top of the ramp. Sergeant Garcia urged the horse forward gently as he took small, tentative steps down into the yard, then past the wall of journalists. Amy showed him Venture's stall and breathed a sigh of relief when the horse was safely inside, away from the snapping cameras.

Sergeant Garcia took off Venture's headcollar and joined Amy outside the stall to answer questions. They all seemed to come at once.

"What can Heartland offer that police vets can't?"

"How long will you be keeping him here?"

"Can you turn this way, please? More to the left," called a TV cameraman.

Amy found herself explaining and re-explaining the work that went on at Heartland, hoping desperately that she was making it clear enough, while Sergeant Garcia answered questions about the night of the storm and Venture's injuries. It was exhausting, and Amy felt like snapping several times; but she followed the sergeant's lead, smiling and nodding, until at last it was over.

"Hope that was bearable for you," said the sergeant when the last journalist had climbed into her car and driven off. "It won't be so bad from now on. Don't be afraid to tell them there's nothing to report."

Now that the barrage of questions was over, Amy felt impressed with the sergeant's calm, professional approach. It had helped a lot. He might seem cool and detached, but he sure knew how to deal with a stressful situation.

He and Amy looked over the half-door at Venture. The sergeant stroked Venture's ears, watching as Amy put a few drops of Rescue Remedy in his water.

"What's that?" he asked.

Amy looked up at him. She guessed he didn't think much of these sorts of remedies, but his curiosity seemed genuine enough. She smiled.

"Bach Rescue Remedy. It's good for sudden change and shock," she explained. "We always give it to new arrivals, to help them settle in." The police horse nosed his water and took a few gulps. "Horses tend to know what's good for them," she said. "That's one of the principles we stand by." She threw the police sergeant another glance, wondering how he'd respond.

Sergeant Garcia shrugged. "Well, I'm sure you'll do your best for him. I'm going to miss him." He stood at the stall door, seeming at a loss. "I'd best get going," he said eventually.

Amy took him to say goodbye to Ty and Lou, then walked

with him towards his car.

"Bye, Amy. I'll be in touch very soon," he said.

"We'll let you know if there's any progress," Amy promised. "And please drop by, any time."

Mark climbed into his car, and Amy watched as he put his key in the ignition. He seemed to be taking his time about it. She wondered if there was something wrong, and was about to step forward when she saw him swat a fly away from his face. She stopped in her tracks, a sudden realization hitting her.

He hadn't been swatting a fly. He'd been wiping away a tear. Slowly, Amy turned and walked back towards the farmhouse.

In the kitchen, Lou and Nancy had almost finished clearing away all the coffee cups. Amy poured herself the dregs from the coffee pot and wandered through into the lounge for a moment, lost in thought. Had she imagined it? Calm, professional Sergeant Garcia? She ran the scene through her mind's eye again. No, she was right. She had seen the glistening tear on his cheek before he brushed it away.

She went back into the kitchen and dumped her mug in the then went out to Venture's stall. He was standing quietly darkness at the back, and shifted nervously when she ed the half-door and stepped inside.

lo there, boy," she said. "It's OK. I'm just going to stroke make you feel a bit better."

ly, so as not to startle him, she reached out and touched ers, then gently began to massage the area with little movements of her fingertips. Venture instantly tensed up. Amy kept on going, moving the circles from his withers up his neck and murmuring to him, but the more she continued to touch him, the more agitated he became. Suddenly, he shifted away from her, and with a jolt of surprise Amy saw fear in the whites of his eyes.

Patiently, she tried again. It was very rare for a horse not to respond to T-touch. She was sure that if she could just keep going steadily for a few moments, he would begin to relax a little. But Venture wouldn't allow it, and Amy began to see tell-tale warning signs that he might be about to react more aggressively: there was growing tension in his neck, and his ears were flattened back. Amy stepped away. There was no point in pushing it.

A shadow fell across the door. It was Ty. "He's one unhappy horse, isn't he?"

Amy nodded. "I can't remember the last horse who wouldn't respond to T-touch," she said. "Maybe we should leave him to settle down a bit longer, and let the Rescue Remedy take effect."

"We could give him some Star of Bethlehem, too," suggeste Ty. "His trauma from the accident obviously goes pretty d It'll help to lift the sense of shock."

Amy looked at Ty, and their eyes locked. They didn't n say it, but they both knew all about the long-lasting eff that night. She leaned her head against the horse's muscled neck, a lump rising in her throat.

"Good idea," she managed to say. "We have to h somehow, Ty."

"We will," said Ty softly. He let himself into the stall, and touched Amy's arm. "Remember all the hours you spent sitting by my bedside, talking to me, begging me to come back. And all the hours you spent helping me after I'd come round. I know you must have despaired sometimes, Amy. I don't know how you found the strength to believe I'd make it. But you did — and now I'm here."

Amy nodded and scrubbed at her face with her sleeve. Ty reached up and laid his hand on the police horse's neck. "So I know you can hold out for Venture, too," he finished. "And this time, I'm right by your side to help you."

After lunch, Amy and Ty went down to the paddocks together to catch Dazzle. For once, there was time for the two of them to go on a trail ride.

Amy watched from the gate as Ty approached the mustang with a halter. She loved watching them working together. When he was being caught, Dazzle was always torn between his love of freedom and his desire to be with Ty, and it could take a few minutes for him to let Ty put on the halter. Ty walked towards him slowly, then turned away as though he had lost interest. Dazzle carried on grazing but Amy could see that he still had his eye on Ty. Gradually, they inched closer until Dazzle submitted and allowed himself to be caught.

"Well done," Amy said with a laugh as Ty led the stallion to the gate. "He's a real tease, isn't he?"

Ty nodded ruefully. "Yeah. But he's never said no altogether — yet."

They led the stallion up towards the front yard. Amy let Ty go on ahead while she fetched her own pony, Sundance, from the barn. Sundance, usually so grumpy with other horses, seemed to have a particular liking for Dazzle. Amy thought it was because he accepted the stallion as leader, so didn't make his usual sneaky moves to assert himself. Whatever the reason, riding Sundance on a trail ride with Dazzle was a pleasure.

They set off up the track towards Clairdale Ridge with Dazzle slightly in front. Both horses were enjoying the bright February afternoon, arching their necks and skittering over the hard ground – especially Sundance, who was kept indoors more over the winter. Ty put Dazzle into a trot and they soon reached the open ground, where they could canter. Ty was still schooling Dazzle so they cantered along very sedately, with Amy and Sundance setting the pace. It was lovely, and as they slowed to a trot, Amy found herself wishing that she and Ty could have more times like this. Other girls with horse-mad boyfriends got to ride out together all the time. If only they could keep Dazzle!

But then she pushed the thought away. There were always new horses to ride at Heartland, and Dazzle wasn't the first that Ty had grown close to. Accepting that things moved on and embracing the new challenges as they arrived was a vital part of what they did. They bonded with horses, then had to let them go.

Thinking about this reminded Amy of Ben. Red was the only horse that he had a strong bond with; he wasn't so interested in any of the others. She turned in her saddle and waited for Ty to ride up alongside her.

"Ben seems really worked up about this show," she commented. "Even more than usual. I get this feeling there's something on his mind."

"I guess it's a big event," said Ty.

"Even so..." Amy trailed off and stroked Sundance's neck. "He didn't want to join-up with Molly," she said. "He's just so preoccupied at the moment. Like he can't concentrate on Heartland at all."

Ty opened his mouth to say something, then seemed to change his mind. "Well, he'll always put Red first," he said. "I don't think we're ever going to change that."

"No," Amy agreed uncomfortably. "I guess not."

Amy didn't want the ride to end, but all too soon, they were clattering back into the yard. Ty untacked Dazzle and took him down to the paddock while Amy settled Sundance back in his stall. She was still thinking about Ben. Perhaps she needed to give him more space to be the person he wanted to be — if she didn't accept him as he was, things were always go   be difficult.

She got a grooming kit to give Sundance a rub-   sink, was soon absorbed in giving his buckskin coat lon   in the sweeps with the body brush.   unbol

A voice interrupted her and she looked up. It was   "He

"Hi, Amy," he greeted her. He seemed uneasy. "Are   you to

Amy gave Sundance's mane a few quick strokes.   Slow the usual," she said. "Why? Is something wrong?"   his with

"Not — not really," said Ben. "It's just t   circling

trailed off and Amy stopped brushing.

"Just what?" she asked gently. "Are you OK?"

"Yes. Yes, I'm fine," said Ben. He took a deep breath. "It's just that I'm thinking of leaving Heartland," he finished in a rush.

Amy dropped the body brush and stared at him.

"Leaving?" she echoed, dumbfounded.

Ben nodded, his blue eyes troubled. "I'm sorry, Amy. I've been thinking it over for weeks. It's not that I don't like the work here, or what you do. It's all fantastic and I've learned loads. You and Ty are both amazing... But it's just not for me. I've realized I want to concentrate on competing."

Amy couldn't quite take it in. "Leaving," she said again, almost in wonderment. Ben looked at her awkwardly.

"So when are you planning on going?" Amy asked.

"I haven't got anything lined up yet," Ben admitted. "I wanted to talk to you first. But I'm going to start looking for a place at a competition yard. That'll be the best way to maximize Red's potential. I really owe it to him, Amy. He could make it to the top, but I can't spend enough time with him here."

Amy felt something twist inside her. She thought of how she had given up competing on her own horse, Storm, because she wanted to put Heartland first – but here was Ben, walking away from it. She forced a smile. "Well. It must have been a difficult decision to make," she managed to say. "I'll be sorry to see you go, Ben. Really sorry. But I guess you have to do what's right for you."

Ben nodded. "Yeah. I'll miss you guys, and everything here –

believe me. I just think that the time has come to move on."

Amy picked up the body brush, trying to push down her feelings. *You can't do this to us,* she wanted to cry. *We need you here. You can't just go!* But instead she smiled again. "Well, I hope you find a good yard," she said. "You're right, you and Red could go all the way to the top."

Ben looked relieved. "Thanks for being so understanding, Amy," he said. "But I'm not disappearing quite yet. It might take a while to find the right place, and anyway, I won't go until you've got someone to replace me. If you decide to, that is."

Amy couldn't bring herself to think that far. "Well, we can talk about that later," she said.

Ben nodded, and headed off. Amy quickly finished up with Sundance, her mind reeling, then took the grooming kit back to the tack room. Ty was in there, giving Dazzle's tack a quick wipe-down. He looked up as she came in.

"What's up?" he asked immediately. "Is it Venture?"

Amy felt herself welling up. "Ben's just told me he's leaving," she said, feeling a tear roll down her cheek. "I can't believe it."

Ty stood up and put his arms around her. "I wondered when he was going to tell you," he said. "I'm glad he has."

Amy stepped back sharply. "You knew?" she exclaimed. "You knew, and you didn't tell me! Ty! How could you?"

"Ben asked me not to," Ty said simply. "He wanted to tell you in his own time."

"But he told you." Amy slumped down on one of the tack room chairs, feeling almost winded – and somehow betrayed. She stared at the wooden floor.

"Hey," said Ty softly. "It's not the way you think it is. Ben knew you'd take it hard. That's why he wanted to be sure before he said anything to you."

Amy looked up and searched Ty's face. His eyes were full of warmth and love for her, and she thought of what he had said earlier, in Venture's stall. He held out a hand and pulled her to her feet.

"Don't feel bad, Amy," he said, gazing into her eyes. "You've still got me, right?"

Amy nodded, trying to stem the tears that were now flowing freely. "I just can't believe it," she said, in a strangled voice. "I ... I thought something was wrong, but I never thought... Ty, it's not my fault, is it?"

Ty looked startled. "Your fault? How on earth could it be?"

Amy bowed her head. Ty drew her close to him and kissed the top of her head. "People move on, just like horses, Amy," he whispered. "That's what Heartland's about, remember? As long as we're holding fast, everything else can change."

By the next morning, Amy felt a bit better. It was Sunday and there was no rush to get ready for school, so she decided to have her morning session with Molly slightly later than usual. She was leading the mare out of her stall when she heard the sound of a car coming up the driveway. She paused, curious. They weren't expecting anyone. Surely it wasn't a reporter, nosing around Venture already!

The car pulled into the yard and a woman in her mid-twenties jumped out. She was small and slender with long fair hair and a golden tan. She approached Amy with a big smile, and Molly gave a whinny of welcome.

Amy realized that this must be Eloise Beatson, Molly's owner. "Hello," she greeted her. "I'm Amy Fleming. You must be..."

"Eloise," said the woman, smiling. She put her arm around Molly's neck and gave her a hug. "It's good to meet you."

Molly nudged Eloise with her nose, her ears pricked. Amy was intrigued to see the mare's happy response to her owner. It was hard to believe that they had any problems at all. "She sure is pleased to see you," she laughed.

Eloise nodded. "I'm missing her so much. I was passing, so I thought I'd drop by to see how she's doing."

"I was just about to take her down to the training ring," said Amy. "Would you like to come and join in?"

Eloise was thrilled at the idea. Amy handed her the lead rope, and watched as horse and owner walked just ahead of her down the track. Was she imagining it, or did Molly seem slightly more nervous today? She was jogging and tugging on the lead rope, which she didn't do when Amy was leading her. Perhaps it was just excitement at seeing Eloise again – but it might be something else.

She caught up with Eloise to walk alongside her. Molly was sweating, and Amy realized she was right. The mare was pleased to see her owner – but she was definitely more jumpy, too.

"Has Molly been playing up with you much?" asked Eloise.

"Not so far," said Amy. "But I haven't been riding her, I've

45

just been working with her from the ground. I want to make sure she trusts me before I go any further."

Eloise sighed. "I was afraid that would happen," she said.

Amy was puzzled. "What d'you mean?"

"I didn't think she'd play up with you," said Eloise. Her hazel eyes looked pained. "I think she blames me for the accident, so she's punishing me by misbehaving. She's probably fine with everyone else."

Amy shook her head. "Horses aren't naturally vindictive," she said. "And Molly's one of the most affectionate horses I've come across. She wouldn't hold a grudge like that. But they can get quite upset if they feel they've lost their trust in someone. Have you ever seen join-up?"

Eloise shook her head, so Amy explained why it was an essential part of Molly's treatment. "When horses are ridden, they place their trust in their rider. They are basically 'flight or fight' creatures, so they protect their hooves and legs at all costs. They won't step into something they can't see clearly, like muddy water or long grass, unless they're sure they're going to get out of it safely. But a trusting horse will do it if his rider asks him to."

"So it's like I said. Molly resents me for taking her through that creek," said Eloise.

"It's not ... resentment," said Amy carefully. "It's more that she needs reassurance. She's very trusting by nature, so her accident was a big blow to her confidence. She doubts her own judgement as much as she doubts you personally."

Eloise looked uncertain. "Well ... I guess that makes sense," she said. "So you're using join-up to teach her to trust again?"

"That's right," said Amy. "I'll join-up with her first, then it would be a good idea if you did it, too."

She took the lead rope from Eloise and unclipped it, then drove the horse away from her around the ring. Eloise retreated to the gate as Amy pushed Molly into making the well-practised choice: to stay on the edge, or come and be with her in the centre of the ring.

"Your turn now," said Amy, walking to the gate with Molly close behind her. She hoisted herself on to the fence to watch Eloise try the technique. "First of all, you have to make yourself the aggressor. Stand big and tall, drive her away from you and keep her moving."

Eloise began to do as Amy said, but without much conviction. Her body language was nervous and she only took a few hesitant steps towards the horse. Molly was unsure what she wanted and wandered away looking confused.

"Really drive her," Amy called. "Use your arms to shoo her away."

Eloise strode more confidently towards her horse. Molly threw up her head and backed off. Eloise stopped. "I can't," she called, biting her lip. "How can it be right to drive her away? She might not come back."

"She will," Amy promised. She jumped down from the fence and went to stand beside Eloise. But as she got closer, she realized to her alarm that the young woman was close to tears.

"She'll come back to you. She won't to me," said Eloise in a trembling voice. "I can't send her away. I really can't."

Suddenly Amy realized that it wasn't only Molly's confidence that had taken a knock. It was Eloise's, too. Horse and owner had got into a spiral of mistrust, with Molly no longer sure that she could rely on Eloise's judgement – or her own. The problem wasn't quite as simple as Amy had thought; she could help Molly to regain her confidence, but unless Eloise regained hers too, they'd soon be back where they started.

Chapter Five

"I think it would help if you drop by whenever you can," Amy told Eloise as they walked back to her car. Amy had taken over join-up and restored Molly's confidence — but not in Eloise.

"Do you really think so?" asked Eloise.

"Yes," said Amy firmly. "It's important that we work with Molly together. We'll gradually build up the things she's willing to do, like walking over small objects or through puddles. By the end of it, you might be happy doing join-up with her, too."

Eloise smiled, still looking a little pale. "I hope so, Amy," she said. "I think you're doing a great job. I don't want to mess it all up."

"She's your horse," Amy reminded her gently. "It's your relationship with her that we need to put back on track. But we'll get there, I promise."

Eloise drove off, and Amy went inside for Sunday brunch. Lou and Ty were already sitting at the table, while Nancy was helping Grandpa serve up scrambled eggs and fried tomatoes. Ben had gone for lunch with his mother, which made it easier to talk about his departure. It had come as a shock to everyone.

"I'll put an ad in the local paper for a replacement," said Lou, pouring more coffee. "And on our web site as well. We'll probably get most responses that way."

"Good idea," agreed Jack. "But I don't imagine we'll be short of applicants."

Amy sat down, suddenly feeling sad again. Ben had been through so much with them all. How could he just walk away?

"You're going to be busy, Lou," said Nancy, handing around slices of toast. "It's not going to be easy, making wedding plans on top of recruiting new staff."

Amy looked at Lou with a jolt, remembering that she too would be leaving when she got married. She felt as though the legs on her chair had given way. Everyone was abandoning Heartland!

"I'm sure I'll cope," said Lou politely.

"Oh yes," said Nancy. "You're very capable. But I'm sure you'll be glad of some help, all the same. I've been thinking – I'd love to make your wedding cake for you. That would be one thing off your list, wouldn't it?"

Lou frowned. "It's a bit soon to be thinking about that, isn't it?" she began.

"Oh no," insisted Nancy. "It's much better to plan things early. I've brought some books for you to look at. You'll want to choose the recipe yourself, I'm sure."

Lou took a deep breath. "Thank you, Nancy," she said, clearly trying her best to be gracious. "I'll take a look when I'm not too busy."

Amy realized she'd been holding her breath and let it out with relief. For the time being, it looked as though Lou was still concentrating on Heartland. Right now, Amy didn't want to face the thought of her sister's mind turning elsewhere.

When Amy got on the school bus the next morning, it felt as though a week had passed, not a weekend. So much had happened — Venture's arrival, Eloise's session with Molly, but above all, Ben's announcement. As Amy sat down next to Soraya, she wondered how her friend would react. She had liked Ben quite a lot before she started going out with Matt.

Soraya launched straight into telling Amy about her weekend — how she and Matt had gone to the movies, how they'd eaten too much ice cream, how they'd walked through the woods on Sunday and thought they'd got lost...

At last she came to an end. "So how was your weekend?" she asked.

Amy looked Soraya in the eyes. "Ben's leaving," she told her.

Soraya gave a little gasp. "Leaving?" she exclaimed. "Amy! But ... why?"

"He wants to move to a competition yard," Amy replied. "So he can concentrate on jumping."

Soraya recovered, and looked thoughtful. "Well, I guess that makes sense," she said matter-of-factly. "Red always meant more to him than anything else. Are you going to get someone else?"

"Lou's putting an ad on our web site," said Amy.

"I bet you'll get tons of responses," said Soraya. "Loads of people would give their eye teeth to work at somewhere like Heartland."

Amy nodded, feeling a little flat. Soraya was taking the news in her stride, as though she'd never given Ben a passing glance.

Everyone seemed to think it was the obvious thing for him to do. Why was it only Amy who felt upset?

It was a relief to leave school behind and get back to Heartland. Over the next few days, Amy concentrated on Molly and Venture. Join-up progressed quickly with Molly, and Amy was soon able to start riding her. At first, the mare was nervous, napping and running backwards whenever she saw a strange object. But the join-up sessions had done their work. With a little reassurance and encouragement, the mare began to put her trust in Amy, and she soon started walking across different surfaces without a problem — through muddy patches, areas strewn with straw, or in between logs laid close together on the ground.

On one evening, Eloise visited again. She was delighted to hear how well the mare had been doing, and as they led Molly down to the training ring, Amy encouraged her to try join-up once more.

"I promise you she'll respond," Amy reassured her. "Just trust in the process. She'll want to join you in the middle of the ring as soon as you let her."

"Well, if you're really sure," said Eloise reluctantly.

"I'm certain of it," said Amy emphatically.

She opened the gate and led the mare into the ring. After showing Eloise how far the mare had progressed with different obstacles, she handed Eloise the lead rope.

"There you go," she said with a grin, backing away towards the gate. "She's all yours."

Amy watched as Eloise took a deep breath, then unclipped the lead rope and drove the mare away from her around the ring.

"Keep it going for a while, until she's giving really clear signals," called Amy.

Eloise gave a determined little nod. She drove Molly on until she was chewing frantically, pleading to be allowed to join her owner. Then, when Eloise slowly turned her back, Molly didn't hesitate. The mare walked over at once to nuzzle her shoulder, and blow gently in her hair. Eloise's face shone with joy, and Amy smiled to herself. It was great to see horse and rider gradually rebuilding their faith in each other.

But work with Venture was not progressing so smoothly. It was difficult to do active work with him, as a lot of movement obviously caused him pain and distress. Join-up was out of the question. Amy had decided to try a mixture of flower treatments and massage to reach the horse, but even that wasn't working. He still seemed to hate T-touch, which Amy found baffling. It couldn't be causing him pain, surely? It was such a gentle technique.

"It's almost as though he's hurting all over," Amy commented one evening, as she and Ty led the police horse slowly down the track for some exercise.

"Yes — in pain and depressed," agreed Ty, as Venture came to a halt.

"Come on, Venture," encouraged Amy, realizing that he had stopped walking altogether.

Venture hung his head and didn't move. When Amy tugged

on his lead rope, he simply stretched out his neck, his nostrils flaring. Ty gave the horse an encouraging nudge from behind, and very reluctantly, Venture stepped forward again.

"I wonder if there's something that all those experts missed," Amy said worriedly. "Something physical, I mean. It's just not normal for him to hate exercise so much, is it? It'd be awful if we were causing more damage."

"We could get Scott to give him another check," suggested Ty. "But like you say, he's had so many examinations already. It's very strange."

They coaxed the horse around one of the paddocks, knowing he would develop other health problems if he stopped moving altogether, then led him back to his stall. Leaving Ty to give him a gentle rub-down, Amy went inside to phone Scott. The sooner the vet came over, the better.

"Do you want to speak to Scott?" Amy asked Lou, picking up the phone. "I'm just calling him."

Lou looked up from the pile of job applications in front of her. "Oh? What about?"

Amy hesitated. "Venture," she said reluctantly. Her sister's doubts about the horse seemed to be growing with each day that passed, and Amy didn't like to admit there wasn't any improvement.

Lou looked concerned. "Amy, Scott's a wonderful vet, but he's not a miracle-worker. Venture's already been seen by every specialist under the sun."

"I know, I know," said Amy hurriedly. "I just want him to give his back another once-over, that's all."

Lou pursed her lips and frowned. "You know, there's one reporter who just won't go away," she said. "She phones almost every day. I keep fobbing her off, but it would be nice to have some good news to pass on."

"It's going to take time. Sergeant Garcia said we shouldn't worry about the media," Amy replied, in a slightly defensive tone. "Do you want to speak to Scott now, or not?"

Lou shook her head, then turned back to the applications. Quickly, Amy punched in the vet's number and asked him to come over — as soon as possible so that they could reassess Venture's treatment, if necessary. When she'd finished, Lou had clearly decided to drop it, because she looked up with a smile.

"We've had quite a few responses to our ad," she said. "D'you want to take a look?"

"Sure!" said Amy, feeling relieved. "Are there any hopefuls?"

"I think so."

Amy sat down next to Lou as she flicked through the applications. There were seven altogether.

"I think these two girls are probably too inexperienced," said Lou, handing Amy the printouts. "Neither of them have actually worked with horses before. They've done a bit of riding. Both horse-mad, of course."

Amy smiled and scanned their applications. "Shame," she said. "But you're right, we need someone who knows what they're doing, at least in terms of stable management."

Lou handed Amy the rest of the papers. "The others all seem like they might be OK," she said. "Take a look."

Amy perused them quickly. There was Jay, who had been a stable lad in a racing stables; Patrick, now retired, who was probably the most experienced of all, having spent his life working with horses; Joni, whose parents ran a Morgan stud farm in Alberta, Canada; Stephanie, who had three years' working experience in a riding stables; and Zoë, who owned a dressage horse.

"She'd be looking to stable him here," Lou pointed out.

"Well, that's OK," said Amy. "We stable Red without a problem. It would be good to meet her."

"What about the others?" asked Lou.

Amy spent a few minutes reading. "I'm not sure about Patrick," she said after a while. "He's experienced, sure. But I'm not sure he'd fit in here. He talks about 'breaking' horses instead of gentling or backing them. It's not a good sign. If he had any real understanding of places like Heartland, he'd know that we think differently. After all, we've been in the press enough times by now!"

Lou's face clouded over at the mention of newspapers and Amy quickly moved on. She scanned the rest of the applications. "I'd like to meet everyone else, though. They all sound like they might fit in. It's so difficult to tell without meeting them."

"So that's Jay, Stephanie, Joni and Zoë," said Lou. "We should discuss it with Ty and Grandpa, then I'll set up some interviews."

"Ty's mom is picking him up early tonight," said Amy. "Maybe we could talk about it over supper tomorrow?"

"Good plan," said Lou. "I'll ask Grandpa if that's OK."

"See you later!" Amy called to Ty and Ben the next morning, heading inside for her shower.

It had been a rush to get everything done, as usual. Amy had spent half an hour with Venture, gently massaging him with diluted lavender oil, but the police horse still wouldn't let himself respond. Amy was glad that Scott had said he would come sometime during that day. She hoped he'd be able to offer some reassurance about his physical condition, at least.

She dived into the shower. Ten minutes later she was bounding down the stairs, her long brown hair still damp.

"Do you want a lift home from school tonight?" asked Lou, as Amy grabbed her coat. "I have to go to the supermarket. I can pick you up, if you like."

"Great," said Amy, wrapping her scarf around her neck. "See you then."

The day dragged. Amy was impatient to know what Ty and Grandpa would make of the applications, and anxious to hear what Scott would think about Venture. She drifted in and out of her own thoughts, and wondered if schoolwork would ever really matter to her as much as it was supposed to. Only rarely, when it was about something that really interested her, such as the environment, did it take over from her thoughts about Heartland.

At last the final bell rang and she was able to head out into the school parking lot to find Lou.

"I've already done the shopping," Lou told her. "Scott phoned just as I was leaving. He was running late, but he should be at

Heartland by the time we get back." She glanced sideways at Amy and grinned. "He's staying for supper."

Amy glanced at the ring on her sister's finger. In some ways, their engagement made no difference at all; Lou and Scott were both so busy that they had little chance to see much more of each other. But that would all change once they were married.

"That journalist called again today," Lou went on, her voice becoming anxious. "I'm running out of things to say."

"They can't expect us to work a miracle in five minutes!" Amy exclaimed. "I'm not going to give up on Venture just because a few journalists keep pestering us, Lou. Think of Ty. We didn't give up on him after the storm, did we?"

"I wasn't suggesting you give up on him," Lou responded quietly. "I just worry, that's all."

Amy lapsed into silence. She knew that Lou was right to be anxious – if only for Venture's sake. She had so little to go on, other than her belief that they had to help him through. And, while she didn't like to admit it, the constant media pressure was beginning to get to her, too.

Scott's pick-up was parked in the front yard when they arrived. Amy helped Lou unload the shopping and staggered into the kitchen with her hands full of shopping bags, Lou just behind her. Scott and Nancy were sitting at the table.

"Hi there!" said Nancy, as they dumped the bags on the kitchen floor. "Do you need some help?"

"No thanks, that's it," said Lou. "What are you two up to?"

Scott looked up and grinned. "Wedding stationery," he said,

going slightly pink. "Nancy's been introducing me to all the possibilities. It's intriguing – a whole new world I never knew about!"

The smile died on Lou's lips. "Oh," she said, leaning down to unpack the carrier bags. "Well, could you move it off the table, please? It's all over the job applications. We're going to be looking at those over supper."

Amy saw the disappointment on Scott's face, and Nancy's puzzled look. "Anyone would think you didn't want to get married, Lou!" she quipped.

Lou straightened up quickly. "That's not true," she retorted. "I just –" She stopped, twisting a can of chopped tomatoes in her hands.

"Wedding nerves," said Nancy knowingly. "Happens to everyone."

Lou looked as though she might explode. For a heart-stopping moment, Amy wondered if her sister was getting cold feet about the whole engagement.

Scott got to his feet. "Hey, sweetheart," he said. "I know there's no hurry. We can take our time mulling things over."

He touched her arm and Lou relaxed. "Sorry," she muttered, resting her head on Scott's shoulder for an instant. Amy saw him smile down at her and realized there was nothing wrong between them. But Lou's reaction still didn't make sense.

"I'll clear everything out of your way," said Nancy. "I need to get going, anyway." She gathered together the stationery samples and dropped them in her bag.

"Aren't you staying for supper?" asked Amy as Nancy shrugged on her thick woollen coat. "Grandpa should be in from the feed market soon."

"No, I was just dropping by with those brochures," said Nancy. "I need to get back home. I'm cooking supper for an old friend of mine. But thanks, anyway. Don't forget to take a look at those cake recipes, Lou!" She gave a quick wave at the door, and was gone.

Amy and Scott helped Lou put away the groceries. Lou disappeared to take toiletries to the bathroom, and when she came back she was her usual composed self.

"I'm ready to take a look at Venture when you are, Amy," said Scott when they'd finished.

"Sure," Amy replied.

They went out to Venture's stall. The police horse was standing at the back, his head drooping. Amy slipped a halter over his head, then led him slowly into the yard. Venture took small, reluctant steps, resisting Amy as she gently pulled on his lead rope.

Scott scrutinized the horse from all angles, then gave him a thorough physical examination, working his way carefully all over his body. When he'd finished, he shook his head, frowning. "I really can't find anything wrong with him. There's no inflammation or swelling in any of the joints. There might be an underlying back problem, but he's had X-rays, and the police would have brought in back experts to check him out. If they didn't find anything..." He shrugged.

Amy stroked Venture's nose, her heart going out to the

suffering horse. "We're trying different flower remedies," she told Scott. "Star of Bethlehem for the original shock of the accident, and Rock Rose to help lift his fear of pain. I'm working with the idea that the memory of pain is as bad as the pain itself, so I keep trying to massage him to help him relax. He hates T-touch, so I just give him a short lavender oil massage every day to lift the anxiety."

Scott nodded. "Sounds good. You could well be right about the memory of pain. But keep looking out for physical clues, too. Slight changes might indicate what the real problem is."

Scott went back to the house. Amy watched him go, feeling frustrated. It felt like all the treatments were no better than a shot in the dark. She thought of Lou's concerns. Perhaps they were going to have to admit defeat with Venture after all.

After putting the horse away, Amy went down to the training ring where Ty was schooling Dazzle. His owners, Mr and Mrs Abrahams, wanted to be able to ride him, but they weren't experienced enough to train him themselves. Amy smiled as she approached the gate. Ty's work was having great results – the stallion was turning into a magnificent riding horse.

This evening, Ty was teaching him how to back up. Amy helped by pushing gently on his shoulders as Ty gave the aids, so that Dazzle understood what was required. By the end of the session, the stallion had willingly taken four steps backwards in a straight line – a major achievement! Happily, Amy and Ty turned Dazzle into his field and wandered up to the farmhouse for supper.

Ben and Scott were already sitting at the table as they walked in, chatting about Ben's plans, while Jack washed his hands at the sink.

Lou was taking pizza out of the oven. "Have a seat," she said. "I'm just about to serve up."

"Looks great," said Ty hungrily.

"Well, tuck in," said Lou, handing out plates. "We'll look at the applications afterwards. You don't have to stick around for that if you don't want to, Ben."

Amy looked across at Ben unhappily. She hated the idea that he wasn't going to be part of things for much longer – it just didn't seem right.

Ben shifted in his seat. "I don't mind. I'd be quite interested, to be honest," he said, looking slightly embarrassed.

So, once everyone had eaten their fill of pizza, Lou handed around copies of the applications. Scott got up and made coffee. There was silence for a while, apart from the rustle of paper, as everyone read through the applications.

"Amy and I had a look earlier," said Lou. "We thought that four of them sounded hopeful – Stephanie, Jay –" she paused to flick through the papers – "Joni and Zoë. We thought the two other girls were too inexperienced, and Patrick was too experienced, in the wrong way. What does everyone else think?"

"I'd agree with that," said Ty. He cast a quick glance at Ben. "The other one I have doubts about is Zoë."

Amy read through Zoë's application again. Her dressage horse, Samurai, featured heavily, and there was a list of the competitions she had won recently. She could see Ty's problem – it was obvious that Zoë already had some serious demands on her time. She drew a deep breath.

"Don't worry about offending me," said Ben. "I can see what you mean. She wants to stable her dressage horse here, so she'll probably have other priorities –" He paused and went red. "Like me."

Ty looked relieved. "Well, yeah, that's what I was thinking," he admitted. "It might be better to have someone who wants to focus on Heartland one hundred per cent. What do you think, Amy?"

Amy was glad that Ben had been so frank. It wasn't easy, discussing what they were looking for with him sitting there.

"You're right," she said awkwardly. "I'm glad you spotted it … and … and thanks for understanding, Ben. We'll go with the other three. Is that OK with you, Grandpa?"

Jack Bartlett nodded and put the papers down. "Yes, that all sounds good to me," he said. "I'm sure one of them will be just what we're looking for."

To her surprise, as they all put the papers down and swigged at their coffee, Amy felt suddenly a lot better. She looked across at Ben. Now that the discussion was over, he had relaxed. It suddenly occurred to her that for him, this wasn't an ending at all. It was a whole new life and a new focus, and it would be amazing to watch his career develop. Amy was sure he'd go far.

And for Heartland, things were going to change, too. What might a new person bring? Amy realized that this was the sort of change she welcomed. There would be new ideas, new input, a whole new atmosphere to explore and enjoy...

It was all a new beginning.

Chapter Six

Sundance had his ears back and was swishing his tail, every inch the picture of a bad-tempered pony. Amy led him back towards his stall, murmuring to him soothingly as she went.

"Come on, boy, it wasn't that bad," she whispered, stroking his mane.

Sundance flicked his ears and grew calmer. Then he butted Amy affectionately, and she laughed.

"In you go," she said, opening the door of his stall. She led him in and slipped off the halter, watching with a smile as the pony headed straight for his haynet and started snatching at it greedily.

"You did a good job, old boy," she told him softly, and walked up to the front yard, where Ty was just bringing Stephanie out of the feed room.

It was Saturday morning. Things had been happening fast over the last few days – all three candidates were keen to attend an interview that weekend, and Stephanie had been the first to arrive. She was tall, with long dark hair pulled back off her face and tied in a ponytail.

"We'll let you know very soon," Amy heard Ty say at the feed-room door.

Amy walked over, smiling. "Are you off now?"

Stephanie nodded. "Thanks so much for showing me

everything. It's really great here," she said. Then she frowned. "I guess you wanted me to spot what the problem is with Sundance. He certainly needs a few good schooling sessions to teach him to respond to commands more promptly. That's what I'd recommend, anyway."

Amy made sure her expression gave nothing away. "Thanks, Stephanie. It's good to hear your impressions," she said. "And thank you for coming. Like Ty said, we'll let you know in the next few days."

Ty escorted Stephanie to her car, then came back to find Amy in the tack room, where she was quickly wiping down Sundance's bridle. He grinned at her. "A few good schooling sessions!" he echoed. "What on earth happened in the training ring?"

"I thought I'd give her Sundance to ride," explained Amy. "You know how grumpy he can be. I guessed it would show how she handles difficult horses."

"And?" queried Ty.

"Sundance clearly didn't think much of her. Her response was to tell me he was playing up, then ask me for a crop." Amy grinned mischievously.

"You didn't give her one, did you?"

"Of course not," said Amy. "I just told her to do what she could with him. She got quite frustrated trying to make him canter, and said he needed teaching a lesson." She frowned. "I don't mind all that – Sundance can be a real brat. It was more that it didn't cross her mind to think of another way of handling the situation, or even to ask me what I thought she should do. You'd think that if she'd done her homework about Heartland, she'd be a bit more open-minded."

Ty nodded. "Yeah. To be honest, she didn't show much interest when I showed her around the feed room. I talked to her about the flower remedies and herbs, but she didn't ask any questions."

Amy sighed. "Oh well. On to the next one. It's Jay, isn't it? The lad whose old stables are closing down?"

"Yes, and he's already here," said Ty. "He arrived early, so I asked Ben to show him around. I think they're down in the barn now."

They walked down the track to find Ben and Jay. As they entered the barn, they heard Ben describing life at Heartland. "All the horses are treated as complete individuals," he was saying. "It's great to see them recover, though, to be honest, you wouldn't be involved in the treatment side that much. Amy and Ty do all that. They're fantastic – the most patient people I've ever met…"

Amy felt touched at hearing his words, but awkward at the same time. Ideally, they did want someone who could help with the treatments. How come Ben had never taken that on board?

Ben stopped when he saw them, grinning self-consciously. "Here they are," he finished. "Amy, this is Jay. Jay, Amy. You've already met Ty, right?"

Jay nodded and stepped forward to shake Amy's hand. He was much smaller than either Ben or Ty, with intense dark eyes and floppy black hair. Amy wondered how he would fit into an environment like Heartland. The racing world was famous for being tough and ruthless with the horses. It seemed unlikely that a stable lad would have the right sort of attitude – but then she pushed the thought away. She would judge him on his own merits.

"I've been showing Jay the stables," said Ben. "I was just about to take him down to see Dazzle, but maybe you'd like to do that."

"Thanks, Ben," said Amy. "Dazzle's paddock is a good place to start!"

Leaving Ben to get on with the stable chores, Ty and Amy showed Jay the way down to the bottom paddock, chatting to him as they went. Jay was fascinated by everything that they did at Heartland, and listened intently when they talked about the alternative methods that they used.

"Some of those herbs would be great with young race-horses," he commented. "It's difficult to calm them down, though I find massaging them helps."

"You use massage?" Suddenly Amy was reminded of Ryan, the stable lad who had been terribly injured rescuing some racehorses from a fire. He had such a special bond with Gallant Prince, the racehorse who had come to Heartland for healing … and Jay had something of the same gentle air about him.

"Yes," said Jay. "I don't know any special method or anything. I just kind of stroke them. It really chills them out."

They reached Dazzle's paddock. The mustang was grazing at the far end, but he raised his head immediately when Ty whistled.

"He's a beauty," said Jay in admiration. "Is he a mustang?"

"That's right," said Ty. He handed Jay a halter. "Could we watch you catch him? Then we'll take him up to the yard."

Jay entered the paddock with the halter hidden behind his back. The stallion stamped a foreleg and snorted. Jay stood quietly for a minute, and didn't stir when Dazzle took a few steps back. Dazzle eyed him again from a safer distance, and Amy could hear Jay murmuring to him in a soft voice. Dazzle flickered his ears, listening. Then Jay turned his back on him and wandered off across the paddock. Dazzle watched him go, looking puzzled. Jay turned to face him once more and carefully stepped towards the stallion. Dazzle allowed him to approach, and without any further fuss, Jay slipped the halter over his head.

Amy smiled as Jay led the mustang to the gate. "That was great," she enthused. "You sure know how to handle horses."

Jay blushed endearingly under his tanned skin. "Well, I work with them every day," he pointed out modestly. "Wouldn't be much use if I hadn't picked up a thing or two by now!"

In the front yard, Ty and Amy watched as Jay brushed the mustang down.

"Shall we give him Dazzle to ride?" Ty asked Amy in a low voice. "It'd be interesting to see how he goes for someone else."

Amy nodded. It was a good idea. Dazzle's schooling was almost finished but he was only used to being ridden by Ty, and sometimes Amy; before he went back to his owners, he would need to behave for more inexperienced riders, and riders who didn't know him well.

"Could you tack him up, please, Jay?" Amy called. "I'll go and get his tack for you."

Dazzle behaved perfectly as Jay tacked him up. He had to stand on a bucket to reach the mustang's ears, but Amy was struck by his deft, soothing movements, and the way he never did anything to upset or startle the stallion. He was a natural. He hoisted himself easily into the saddle, and Amy and Ty walked alongside him as he rode the mustang down to the training ring.

It was there that things stopped going quite so smoothly. Amy asked Jay to take Dazzle through some figure of eights and serpentines, then over some trotting poles, and it soon became clear that he was unaccustomed to this type of riding. Before starting, he shortened both his stirrups and his reins, then urged Dazzle forward with quick, sharp nudges of his heels. Dazzle quickly got confused and came off the bit, poking his nose in the air and hollowing his back.

Ty grimaced. "I think we should stop him," he said to Amy in a low voice. "I don't want to have to do a complete reschooling!"

"That's enough, Jay!" called Amy hastily. "Thanks. Can you come back over here?"

Jay rode over looking flustered. "We don't really do this kind of stuff," he said. "But I'm sure I could learn."

Amy smiled encouragingly at him. "That's OK. We'll take Dazzle in now," she said, avoiding the issue for the time being. "Ty will show you around the rest of the yard and talk you through all the herbs and other remedies that we use."

Jay looked enthusiastic. "OK, that's great," he said, dismounting.

Amy took Dazzle's reins and the three of them walked back up to the yard. Amy felt really disappointed that Jay's riding wasn't what they were looking for. He had such a gentle touch – perhaps they could train him up on the riding side? But realistically, it would take too much time to teach him from scratch. She sighed. Finding someone to replace Ben wasn't going to be as straightforward as she'd imagined.

Over lunch, Amy and Ty discussed Jay's interview while Lou and Grandpa listened.

"He was so interested in all the remedies," said Ty regretfully. "He hadn't come across many of them before, but he was so enthusiastic. He'd learn that side of things quickly enough, but his riding..." He shook his head.

"Just not up to it," agreed Amy. "We wouldn't be able to let him do any of the exercising, or at least not with horses that needed schooling. It's a real shame. He'd be fantastic around the yard."

"Well," said Lou. "That sounds like another rejection to me."

They all looked up as they heard a gentle knock on the door. Lou frowned. "We're not expecting another candidate yet, are we? I hope it's not a reporter!"

Amy shook her head. "Not for another half-hour or so. Maybe Joni's early." She went to answer the door. "Sergeant Garcia!" she exclaimed.

"Hello, Amy," said the sergeant. "I thought I'd drop

by on my day off. Hope you don't mind."

"No! No, that's fine," said Amy, but her heart was sinking. "Would you like to come in for a moment, or see Venture right away?"

Sergeant Garcia hesitated. "I think I'd like to see him, if you don't mind," he said.

"That's fine. I'll just get my coat," said Amy, forcing a smile. How on earth was she going to tell him that they'd made no progress with Venture at all?

Chapter Seven

"I'm afraid we haven't really got very far with him yet." Amy opted for the truth as they approached Venture's stall. "I'm sure we will, but it's going to take time."

Sergeant Garcia didn't look surprised. "I wasn't expecting anything," he said. "I just thought I'd drop in to see him, that's all."

At the sight of his colleague, Venture's ears pricked forward and he gave a whinny of welcome. Sergeant Garcia stepped forward to stroke his neck, and the horse nuzzled him affectionately.

Amy was momentarily filled with hope. "Do you think he seems any better?" she asked.

Mark Garcia shrugged. "Difficult to tell, to be honest," he said. "He's always given me a welcome, even just after the accident." He stepped back and studied Venture more carefully. "He's not the horse he was, I'm afraid. We could walk him out in the yard, if you want me to check for progress."

Amy nodded, but her hope had died again. If Venture's welcome hadn't been anything new, she was sure that nothing else had changed either. She went to fetch a halter from the tack room and headed back to Venture's stall. Just as she was about to go back inside, she stopped.

Mark had cupped one arm under the horse's head and was

resting his forehead against Venture's cheek, gently stroking his muzzle with his other hand. His face, usually so calm and controlled, was etched with pain and sadness.

"Poor old boy," she heard him murmur. "When are you going to come back to me, eh?"

Amy drew in her breath. She swallowed, and stepped back for a moment to collect herself. The words were so painfully familiar. *When are you going to come back...* She felt choked. What with Ben leaving and all the interviews, had she lost sight of Venture's predicament? Of course, they'd still been treating him. But Mark's words reminded her of how it had been with Ty – the long days, weeks, that had stretched out without any hope...

She cleared her throat, and stepped forward once more. The sergeant looked up, quickly readjusting his expression, and smiled as Amy came back into the stall. Unsure what to say, she slipped the halter over Venture's head and led him out into the yard.

Venture moved with all his usual reluctance, and after one painful circuit, it was clear that Mark's presence hadn't made any real difference to him at all.

Mark watched him, shaking his head. "Poor old Venture," he muttered. "I guess he's reached the end of the road."

Amy was horrified at the resignation in his voice. "Oh, please don't say that!" she exclaimed. "Sergeant Garcia, you mustn't give up."

The police officer looked at Amy in surprise. "I mustn't give up?" he queried.

Amy felt momentarily embarrassed. Mark Garcia was so dignified and professional. She could tell he'd hate it if he knew that she had seen his pain. She hesitated.

"It's just that... Well, I kind of understand," she said.

Mark Garcia raised an eyebrow. "You understand?" he echoed.

Amy felt tongue-tied, and played with Venture's lead rope.

"Go on," said Sergeant Garcia. "You must mean something by that."

Amy nodded. "Well, yes," she said. "You weren't the only one to have an accident that night." She glanced at him quickly, trying to gauge his reaction. His expression was now intense, and a little muscle worked in his jaw. "Our back barn roof collapsed," she went on. Her voice trembled. "There were horses inside. One of them was killed. And Ty was inside, too." She raised her head. "Ty was in a coma for weeks. I almost despaired, so many times. I just had to wait, and wait..." She paused. "So you see, I do understand."

Sergeant Garcia's face was still. There was a silence, then he reached out and laid his hand on Venture's neck. The big police horse was standing lethargically, resting one hind leg, but he shifted at his rider's touch.

"I..." Mark began. His voice cracked, and he stopped to clear his throat. "I didn't know. Thank you for telling me." He stroked Venture's neck for a moment, his face hidden. Then he sighed, and turned back to Amy. "Venture came here as a last resort. You knew that, didn't you?"

Amy nodded.

"I had lost the strength to believe we'd find a cure for him," he admitted. "Sometimes you just have to accept that things are over. After all, no police horse's career lasts for ever. When one of the vets suggested sending him here, I didn't allow myself to believe it would make any difference."

Amy swallowed. "Well, it hasn't. Yet," she acknowledged humbly. "But I really believe we can reach him, in time."

Mark Garcia nodded, but didn't look convinced.

Amy searched his features. All she could see was deep, unhappy resignation. "You will let us keep on trying, won't you?"

Sergeant Garcia stared at his feet. "That's what I'd like," he said eventually. "The problem is, my bosses can't justify the funds involved in keeping him here indefinitely. But if you think there's a chance…" He looked up, his glance questioning.

"Oh yes," said Amy quickly. "There's always hope. I believe that, I really do. I've had to."

Mark nodded, but his eyes didn't reflect her optimism. "Well. That's something," he said, with a little smile. "Leave it with me. Perhaps we can find a way."

He watched as Amy coaxed the police horse back into his stall, then leaned on the half-door, his chin cupped in his fist. Amy wasn't sure what else to say. The sound of a car pulling up in the yard reminded her that the final candidate was due. She let herself out of the stall and caught a glimpse of a blonde-haired girl getting out of a taxi.

"I'm afraid I have a meeting now," she said awkwardly. "But please stay with Venture as long as you like."

Sergeant Garcia nodded. "Yes, I'll stick around for a while, if you don't mind."

Amy took a deep breath and went to join Ty, who was already shaking hands with the candidate. Amy reminded herself of her name – Joni Janssen, from Alberta, Canada. Unless she'd been staying locally, she'd come a long way, so Amy realized she must be very keen, if nothing else.

"Hi, I'm Amy," she greeted the girl. "You must be Joni. I hope you're not too tired after your journey!"

"Hi, Amy," said Joni. Her blonde, straight hair was cut square halfway up her neck so that it swung around her face, and her grey eyes had a mischievous twinkle in them. "I'm fine, thank you. I stayed with my uncle in Baltimore last night, so it wasn't so far to come."

Amy warmed to her at once. Her accent was subtle – a gentle mix of Canadian and something more lilting. They began to show her around the front yard. When they came to Venture's stall, Amy introduced Sergeant Garcia. Feeling slightly self-conscious, Amy explained why Venture had come to Heartland, with the sergeant listening gravely.

Joni's face filled with sympathy. "My mom had a horse that was involved in an accident. It took so long for him to get better. But he did in the end. Mom always says that time's the greatest healer."

The sergeant responded to the warmth in her voice and Amy saw a gleam of hope light up his eyes. There was something about Joni that meant you couldn't help feeling cheerful, as if she lit up her surroundings with positive energy.

They moved on to Molly's stall. Curious as ever, the pretty mare had been watching their progress around the yard from over her half-door, and she whickered as they approached.

"She's lovely, but she's had a big knock to her confidence recently," Amy explained. "So I'm working on building her trust again, alongside her owner Eloise. She's lost some of her confidence, too – that's part of the problem."

Joni reached up and scratched Molly behind the ear. "Do you use Bach flower remedies at all? I think I'd give her some Larch remedy. It's really good for restoring lost confidence."

Amy felt pleasantly surprised. "That's exactly what I'm giving her!" she exclaimed.

Joni grinned. "My mom swears by those remedies," she said. "I've only learned some of them so far, though."

"That's great," said Amy. "Do you know about other herbal remedies, too?"

Joni shook her head. "Just the Bach ones at the moment. But if there are others that you use here, I'd love to learn them."

Amy exchanged glances with Ty. He smiled, and she knew that they both had a good feeling about Joni. They asked her to give Molly a quick groom so that they could see some of her yard skills. As she did so, she told them a little more about herself. She was seventeen, born in Canada, but her mother was Norwegian and her father Norwegian-American, which meant that she had American citizenship as well.

"I've finished high school, but Mom wants me to carry on studying," Joni explained, expertly picking up one of Molly's feet. She paused to concentrate while she cleaned out the frog, then put the hoof down again and patted the mare to reassure her.

"I'd much rather just start working," she carried on. "I don't want to take a big break from being around horses. I wouldn't mind working with Mom on the stud farm, and carry on with some practical courses I'm doing, but I wouldn't get to do much riding – and I think she'd pressure me into studying more, anyway. But I figure that if I get a good job really soon, somewhere fantastic like here –" she grinned at Ty and Amy – "she'd let me take it, since I'd still be learning."

She finished off with Molly and gave her a kiss on the nose. Ty led the mare back into her stall while Amy took Joni to the tack room.

"We're going to give you Sundance to ride," Amy told her, lifting his saddle from the rack. "Could you take this?"

Joni hoisted the saddle on to her arm, then swung the bridle over her shoulder. Amy led her to Sundance's stall and asked her to tack him up. Amy expected him to be doubly grumpy at being tacked up twice in the same day. She suppressed a smile as Joni led him out of his stall. His whole posture suggested outrage. He dragged his feet and put his ears back, snorting in protest. But Joni took no notice, and tacked him up swiftly.

By the time Joni had ridden Sundance down to the training ring, the pony was beginning to realize that she wasn't going to put up with any nonsense. Whenever he started to hunch his back and resist, Joni sat down deep in the saddle and drove him on. Soon, he had settled on to the bit and was performing perfect circles in a balanced, rhythmic trot.

"He's a character, isn't he?" Joni commented when Amy called her over to the gate. "I wouldn't have thought he had any real problems, though."

Amy laughed. "He doesn't," she admitted. "He's my own pony. He can be a bit grumpy, that's all — but you handled him perfectly. Well done!"

By the end of the day, Amy felt exhausted. Meeting people and talking to them was even more tiring than working with the horses! But as she sat down to eat supper, there was little doubt in her own mind that they had found the ideal replacement for Ben.

Nancy had come over to cook supper. It was a feast of roast vegetables and lamb, and Amy tucked in hungrily. As everyone ate, she and Ty described all three interviewees, so that Grandpa and Lou had a clear idea of what had happened. Ben chipped in with his impressions, and agreed that Joni stood out from the other two by a long way.

"It's a shame about Jay," said Amy. "He was so good around the horses. I hope he finds somewhere else soon."

"He will, I'm sure," said Ty. "We can give him some positive feedback. But he definitely needs to improve his riding skills if he's going to work somewhere like Heartland."

Jack nodded. "Yes, it would be good to give him some encouragement, at least," he said. "So it's Joni that you want. But didn't you say something about her living in Canada?"

"That's the only problem," admitted Amy. "She'd have to leave home, and she needs to start work pretty much straight away."

She shot a glance at Ben. Joni starting work in the near future would put pressure on him to find a competition yard — Heartland couldn't afford to let them overlap for long. He might have to leave earlier than he'd planned. But how could they say that to him?

"And she's how old? Seventeen?" asked Grandpa. "I think in that case, it would be up to us to find her somewhere to live. We can't really expect her to sort all that out for herself."

Nancy stood up and started clearing away the plates. "Well," she said. "I would have thought there's an obvious answer to that. She could live here, couldn't she? I'm happy to help out with the cooking and cleaning, so the extra housework wouldn't be a problem. It might be rather nice for you all."

"Live here?" Amy echoed. For a moment, she felt excited. She had liked Joni so much! It would be great to have her living at Heartland. But there was a big problem. "There isn't a spare room," she pointed out.

Nancy looked puzzled. "Yes, there is."

Amy stared at her. There was only one room that wasn't slept in. And that room had belonged to Marion, her mother. Amy's heart started thudding. Nancy surely wasn't suggesting they used that! She looked across at Grandpa in alarm, hoping that he'd say it wasn't possible. But he had an uncertain expression on his face that Amy couldn't read.

Nancy smiled. "And with everything that's happening," she added, looking at Lou, "there'll soon be two spare rooms, won't there?"

At this, Lou got to her feet. Her face was like thunder. "How dare you!" she shouted. "First you interfere with my wedding plans and all the housework and the cooking and just about everything else, and now you're telling us how to run Heartland! Where Joni lives is none of your business and neither is our mother's room. You've no idea what that means to me and Amy, or to Grandpa!"

She stopped, her voice trembling. Amy's mouth dropped open in shock. She looked at Nancy, who had gone deathly pale. Amy saw that her knuckles, clutching the dirty plates, were white.

There was a silence. Everyone looked stunned. Amy was astonished at Lou's outburst. Her sister had seemed a bit annoyed with Nancy at times, but nothing like this! After what seemed like an eternity, Nancy placed the plates carefully on the draining board and turned back to the table.

"Actually, Lou," she said, "I have a very good idea of what that room might mean to you." She walked quickly to pull her coat off the hook, shrugged it on, and picked up her bag. "I don't think I should come to Heartland for a while," she said quietly, looking at Jack. She opened the door and walked out.

The instant she had gone, Grandpa seemed to pull himself together. He got to his feet and followed her out. Amy heard the sound of Nancy's car starting, then the engine idling for a few minutes before the car headed down the driveway. Everyone sat tensely, waiting for Jack to return. When he appeared in the doorway, he stood still, his face clouded with anger. No one else moved.

"I have no idea why you said what you did, Lou," said Jack. "I simply can't imagine what provoked it. I suppose there must be something; but I'm deeply disappointed in you. In fact, I've never been more disappointed in my life."

Chapter Eight

The mood in the yard was subdued the next morning. It was Sunday. Amy had got up as usual to work with the horses, but there was no sign of Lou. She rode Molly down to the training ring and gave her a basic schooling session, reinforcing the work that they had done so far. She wasn't in the mood for trying anything new with the mare today.

It had been awkward after Grandpa had come back in. Lou had gone straight to bed, followed shortly by Jack, while Ty and Ben had made their excuses and left. Amy decided to ask Lou out on a trail ride that afternoon to cheer her up.

She rode back up to the yard and tied Molly outside her stall. As she began to untack her, Ben stuck his head over Red's half-door.

"Hi Amy," he called. "Can I have a word when I've finished with Red?"

"Sure," Amy called back. She wondered what he wanted to talk about. The situation with Joni was tricky — they still hadn't resolved what to do about her accommodation, and Amy didn't want to upset Ben by asking him to leave early.

Ten minutes later, Ben reappeared and leaned over Molly's half-door.

"I had an idea," he said, as Amy brushed Molly's mane. "There's a spare room in the house where I live. I talked to my landlady last night, and she's willing to rent it. Joni could move in there."

Amy stopped brushing. "Really?" Her heart gave a bound of hope, but she looked at Ben doubtfully. "Are you sure?"

"Yes, it should be fine," said Ben. "Then I can drive her to work, no problem. She'll probably get her own car pretty soon, though, won't she?"

"I guess," said Amy. Then she frowned. Ben was talking as though he'd be working alongside Joni, but there wasn't the money to pay two sets of wages. How could she say that to Ben? He had every right to stay for as long as he needed to.

She hesitated. "Wouldn't you find it a bit much, living and working with the person who's going to take your place?"

"I've thought it all through, Amy," said Ben. "Lou mentioned there's a problem about paying both of us, and I'm happy to let her take over even if I don't have somewhere else to go. Joni's cool. I'm really pleased you've found someone you like. I'll be happy to help her settle in for a few days, then leave. I could still drive her here, though. It's not far."

Amy felt a pang of guilt. Ben was bending over backwards to make everything easier for her, and for Heartland. But perhaps if he'd felt more included, he wouldn't be leaving in the first place.

"What about Red?" she asked. "You don't have a yard to move him to."

"Don't worry," said Ben. "I'll stable him with my aunt until I find somewhere. I've already asked her if there's room."

"You really have thought about everything, haven't you?" said Amy, feeling a strange mixture of sadness and relief.

"It's really good of you, Ben. I'll miss you."

"I'll miss you too," said Ben. He ran a hand through his hair, his expression suddenly miserable. "And everyone else. It might look as though I'm getting everything sorted, but, well, at the moment, it doesn't feel like it."

Amy felt a lump rising in her throat. *You don't have to go*, she wanted to say. But she pushed the thought away. Things had moved on way beyond that. "You know you can come back and visit anytime, don't you?" she asked.

Ben nodded. "Thanks." He gave a little smile. "Just try keeping me away!"

Amy finished with Molly and went indoors. Grandpa was cooking Sunday brunch as usual, but it seemed odd to see him at the oven by himself. Amy realized she'd grown used to seeing Nancy bustling around the kitchen, joking with him.

She told him about Ben's solution for Joni. "It means she can start as soon as she likes," she said.

"Sounds ideal," agreed Jack, taking some eggs from the fridge. "Well, perhaps we could let her know today."

Amy nodded. "I hope so. She was really keen. I'll speak to Lou about it."

There was still no sign of her sister. Amy went upstairs and knocked on her door. "Lou?" she called softly. "It's me. Can I come in?"

She heard a faint "yes", and opened the door. Lou was sitting on her bed, holding a magazine. But Amy wasn't fooled. She guessed that her sister had shut herself away to think.

"It looks like we've sorted out the Joni problem," Amy told her. "She can go and live with Ben — there's a spare room in his house."

Lou ran both hands through her short blonde hair, then let them drop by her side on the bed. "That's good," she said. "Have you called her yet?"

"No. I thought you'd probably need to do it, so you can sort out her contract and everything," said Amy.

"I can deal with all that later. You tell her, if you like."

"OK. Thanks." Amy grinned, then stood in the doorway feeling awkward. "Um ... I was wondering if you felt like coming on a trail ride this afternoon? It's a nice day and a couple of the horses need some exercise."

Lou gave Amy a grateful look. "That sounds good," she said. "Something to blow away the cobwebs."

Amy nodded. "Will you be coming down for brunch?"

Lou smiled. "Yes. I'll see you in a bit." She hesitated, then added, "Thanks, Amy."

Amy ran back downstairs and sifted through the sheaf of applications to find Joni's cellphone number. She dialled it quickly, feeling excited.

"Hi, Joni," she said when Joni answered the phone. "It's Amy here, from Heartland."

"Amy!" said Joni.

Amy could hear a mix of nervousness and anticipation in the girl's voice, and smiled to herself. It was great to be giving her good news. "We'd like to offer you the job, if you're still interested."

"Still interested? Am I ever!" cried Joni. "Oh, thank you. Thank you. That is the best news ever. I can't believe this is happening to me. How soon can I start?"

"Well, we've managed to sort out some of the practical stuff already, so I think you could pretty much start when you like," said Amy, and explained the arrangements that Ben had suggested. "You'll need to sort out the details of your contract with Lou, though."

"That's fantastic," enthused Joni. "I'll just need to check it all out with my mom. I'll call you back, is that OK?"

"Fine," said Amy. "I hope she's happy for you to come here. I think you'll fit in really well."

Over brunch, Amy chattered about Joni's arrival, aware that Lou and Grandpa were both much quieter than usual. Ben told everyone about his plans to go back to his Aunt Lisa's yard for a while.

"She should be able to help me find a competition yard," he said. "She's got lots of contacts. She said she'd be interested to see how I've been training Red, too. I think I'm a lot gentler with him than I used to be."

Amy and Ty exchanged glances. It seemed so long since Ben had arrived. At first, he and Ty hadn't got on at all – especially when Ty had seen how harsh Ben could be with his horse. But things had changed as they'd grown to understand each other. Ben had learned to coax the best out of Red by encouraging him and seeing him as a partner, rather than bullying him. Then, when Ty had first returned to Heartland after being in a coma, Ben had patiently and tirelessly helped him regain his strength. They were now the best of friends.

The phone rang. Lou went to answer it. When she returned to the table, she had a broad smile on her face.

"Joni can definitely come and work here," she announced, sounding much more cheerful than she had earlier. "She arrives on Wednesday."

"Jasmine's obviously glad to be out!" commented Amy that afternoon as she and Lou rode up the track away from Heartland. "She's going really well for you."

"D'you think so?" asked Lou, looking gratified. She was still in the process of regaining her confidence around horses, after not riding for years. She pushed Jasmine into a trot and Amy followed on Snowdrop, another recent arrival, sent to Heartland for reschooling after recovering from an injury. After ten minutes of trotting steadily, Lou looked a lot happier than she had when leaving the yard. Amy brought Snowdrop up alongside her, and the sisters rode along in silence for a few minutes.

Amy wondered how to get Lou talking about the problems that were hanging in the air. She was still baffled by her sister's outburst. There must be all sorts of stuff that Amy hadn't picked up on, and she felt bad for not being more sensitive. Was it about the wedding? Or just about Nancy?

"So … are you still going to let Nancy bake your cake for you?" she asked Lou eventually.

Lou stiffened. "I don't know yet."

"You do still want to get married, don't you?" asked Amy. It didn't feel like quite the right thing to say, but she was grasping at straws.

"Amy!" Lou exclaimed. "Of course I do."

Her voice shook slightly, and Amy looked across at her in concern.

"Scott's not the problem. I really love him," said Lou in a low voice. She looked down at Jasmine's reins, and Amy suddenly realized that she was close to tears. "It's Mom," Lou carried on in a strangled voice. "I ... I just can't bear the thought of her not being there when I get married."

Of course! It was so obvious that Amy couldn't believe it hadn't occurred to her before. "Oh, Lou," she said softly. "I wish I'd realized."

She brought Snowdrop to a halt and gave him a long rein so that he could graze. Lou did the same with Jasmine, impatiently brushing a tear from her eye.

"There's no reason why you should," Lou said. "I didn't know I was going to feel this way until it happened. And Nancy... To be honest, I'm not sure why she does my head in so much. She just does. She keeps sticking her nose in. Nearly every day she comes in going on about brochures or recipes or dresses or caterers – and I don't even know what kind of thing I want yet!"

She paused, fiddling with her reins. "Sometimes," she went on, "when she's putting me under pressure to sort things out, I feel like she can't wait for me to get out so she can take my place."

"Take your place?" echoed Amy, dismayed. "She could never do that!"

But as she spoke, Amy felt a pang of guilt. She had actually been enjoying having Nancy around. She was a wonderful cook, and it was somehow comforting to have an older woman in the farmhouse... And then it struck her.

"Maybe it's something else, Lou," she said cautiously. She took a deep breath. "You don't think that maybe Nancy's doing things that Mom would have done?"

Lou looked up at Amy, tears still welling in her blue eyes. "I don't want her taking anyone's place!" she burst out, and a large tear of rage rolled down her face. "Not mine or Mom's or anyone's! I just want everything to stay the same."

Amy felt tears flooding her own eyes. "So do I," she admitted quietly. "I don't want you to go. I'll miss you so much."

"Maybe you won't miss me," said Lou. "Maybe I'll go and you won't even notice the difference, with Grandpa and Nancy running everything."

Amy shook her head. "It won't be like that, Lou," she said. "Heartland could never be the same without you. But the thing is, you'll be really happy with Scott. And Mom would have wanted that. She'd have been glad to see you move on. She really would."

Lou took a deep breath and rummaged in her pocket for a tissue. She blew her nose, and nodded. "I guess you're right," she said.

Amy gathered up Snowdrop's reins again and they rode on.

"You know, Nancy's not so bad," Amy said after a while. "Remember how I wouldn't accept Lily and Helen as part of the family in Australia? Maybe you've got the same kind of problem with Nancy."

Lou gave a small smile. "Maybe."

"I can understand how you feel, though," said Amy. "I couldn't believe it when she suggested giving Mom's room to Joni."

"I know. That was when I snapped." Lou blushed. "I guess I shouldn't have let her get to me. She's made a big difference to Grandpa."

"He's been a lot happier recently," Amy agreed. She hesitated. "Maybe Nancy's trying to be involved with us all to please him. It must be weird for her if she's never had a family of her own."

"Could be. I hadn't thought of it like that," said Lou. She shrugged. "Well, I'll make an effort from now on. Even if it's just for Grandpa's sake. But that doesn't mean I'm going to start sitting down making cosy wedding plans with her all the time."

"I don't think she'll be expecting you to," Amy pointed out. Lou blushed again. She obviously realized she had some apologizing to do, and Amy began to wish she hadn't rubbed it in. She avoided saying anything else by shortening Sundance's reins and kicking him forwards.

They cantered along the ridge in the crisp winter air, both horses snorting in delight at the chance to stretch their legs.

"Maybe we could take some flowers to Mom's grave

92

sometime soon," Amy suggested when they slowed to a walk again. "We could tell her all about Australia. And if you tell her about getting engaged to Scott, that might make you feel a bit better."

Lou nodded. "That would be good." She sighed. "You know, Amy, it's really not that I don't want to get married. I just don't want to rush anything. So much has happened in the last couple of years. I want to be sure that everything has fallen properly into place before I make another big move."

"That makes sense," said Amy. She was glad that she understood Lou's concerns at last – and she couldn't help but feel relieved that her sister wouldn't be disappearing just yet. "You know, Lou, Mom would have been so happy about you and Scott," she added. "She had tons of respect for him. I'm sure she would have thought it was the right thing."

Lou smiled. "I'm glad you think so."

"I'm sure of it," Amy said firmly. "I really am."

It felt so much better to have things out in the open, and Lou and Amy rode back to Heartland in comfortable silence. Back in the yard, Amy went to check on Venture, thinking of Sergeant Garcia's visit the day before. She felt strangely touched and honoured that she had been able to see past his professional exterior to the pain that lay just beneath. It would be so wonderful to return Venture to him, just as Ty had been returned to her.

She found Ty in Venture's stall, fiddling with the light bulb.

"I've changed it to an orange one," he explained to Amy,

holding up the old bulb. "It'll be a lot more restful for him."

His voice was flat, and as he pocketed the old bulb and unbolted the stall door, he seemed strangely preoccupied. Amy rested her hand on the half-door, frowning, as Ty walked away, his shoulders hunched. She knew him so well. Instinctively, she ran after him and touched his elbow. "Hey. Are you OK?" she asked.

Ty stopped, and shrugged. "Fine," he said.

"Are you sure? It's not ... working with Venture, is it?"

Ty gave a little smile, and shook his head. "No. It's not Venture."

Amy felt relieved. Ty had been as good as his word with the police horse; he had responded to him just like any other Heartland patient. She searched his face. "There is something, though, isn't there?"

Ty sighed. "Well, OK," he admitted. "The Abrahams phoned about Dazzle. I explained how far I'd got with him, and they'd like to take him home. They're not so concerned about his schooling now because they've decided to mainly use him as a stud horse."

"Oh, Ty," said Amy. "I'm sorry. You'll miss him so much. When are they coming for him?"

"This evening," said Ty flatly.

"Today!" Amy exclaimed. "That's so sudden."

"I know. They'll be here in about an hour."

Ty looked wretched, and Amy's heart went out to him. She touched his arm. "You know when we went out on that trail ride together, with you on Dazzle and me on Sundance? I found myself wishing that Dazzle was yours, and that we could ride out together on our own horses all the time…" She hesitated. "Would you like your own horse, Ty? You've never had one. I've got Sundance, and I had Storm, too. But you've always had to say goodbye to the horses you work with."

Ty smiled. "I've never wanted that, Amy. I've always been more interested in healing horses and watching them move on. Dazzle is special because working with him was so much part of me getting better after the accident. But I still have to let him go. It's just harder than usual this time."

"I guess," said Amy, a realization slowly dawning on her, "Dazzle reminds you more of the accident than Venture ever could."

Ty drew in a deep breath. "Well, not so much the accident itself," he said slowly. "To be honest, I don't remember much of what happened that night. But Dazzle's been a big part of the struggle to pull through, yes." His green eyes looked intensely into Amy's. "You know, Amy, it wasn't me who was brave when we took on Venture. I wasn't the one who had to wait and wait, not knowing if things would ever improve."

Amy flushed slightly. "That's what Soraya said, at the time," she admitted. "But I'm not the one waiting for him. Not really. It's so much worse for Sergeant Garcia."

"But you know how he feels," said Ty. "You understand what he's going through."

Amy nodded and raised her eyes to Ty's, a wave of emotion rising through her. She took a deep breath. "I'll make sure I'm around, when the Abrahams come for Dazzle."

"Thanks," said Ty. He smiled. "It's good to know that neither of us have to hold fast on our own any more."

Dazzle pricked his ears, his nostrils flaring, when the Abrahams pulled into the yard with their trailer.

"You've done an amazing job with him!" exclaimed Mrs Abrahams, when Ty led him forward. "He's such a beauty. We can't wait to see what his first foals will be like."

"I'm sure they'll be gorgeous," said Amy.

"Say, maybe we could send you one of them for training?" said Mr Abrahams. "We know how good you are now. I would never have guessed that Dazzle could be so easy to handle."

Amy thought of Daybreak and Solly, two of the young horses she had helped to train. They had both gone back to their owners before she'd had a chance to take them through all the stages of schooling. It would be so exciting to train a foal from the beginning. "That would be fantastic," she said. "Please do."

She watched as Ty guided Dazzle up the ramp. Dazzle was understandably nervous – after all, the last time he had seen the inside of a trailer was when he was still terrified of human contact. But his trust in Ty was absolute. With a little gentle coaxing, the stallion stepped up into the dark interior.

Amy felt a lump grow in her throat as she saw Ty give the stallion a final hug, and murmur something in his ear. He came back down the ramp, and Amy held out her hand. Ty squeezed it as Mr Abrahams did up the bolts.

"Nothing ever stays the same, does it?" Amy whispered to

him, as the Abrahams gave a final wave and climbed into the cab.

"No," Ty whispered back. "But you know what? I really think that's OK."

Chapter Nine

"Amy! Joni's here!" Lou shouted up the stairs.

"I'm coming!" called Amy, pulling on her jeans.

It was Wednesday evening, and Joni had arranged to come straight to Heartland for supper before going to see her new lodgings with Ben.

Amy bounded down the stairs and headed outside, where she found Ty and Ben showing Joni around the yard again. She had stopped at Molly's stall and was giving her a lot of fuss, which she was clearly enjoying.

"Hi, Joni," Amy greeted her. "Good to see you!"

"Hi!" said Joni. "I'm just meeting all the horses again. It's going to be great, getting to know them. I think I'm firm friends with Molly already."

"Can we drag you away from her for supper?" asked Amy, laughing.

Joni grinned. She gave Molly a final pat on the neck and straightened the mare's forelock. Then everyone piled inside to eat.

Jack was helping Lou to serve. The atmosphere between them had improved over the last few days, and Amy guessed that Lou had apologized to him, at least. But Nancy still hadn't been back.

"You'll have to tell me about all the horses, and what you're doing with them," said Joni, enthusiastically tucking into Lou's cheese and potato pie. "Then I'll see how much I can remember in the morning!"

Amy and Ty took it in turns to explain which horses were Heartland residents, and which had come for treatment. Ben chipped in every now and again, explaining where he was able to help out.

Joni listened avidly. "I can't wait to start," she declared. "What time do you get here in the morning, Ben?"

"You don't need to worry about getting here early tomorrow," said Jack. "You'll need time to settle in to your new place."

"Oh, I don't care about that," said Joni cheerfully. "I'd much rather come with Ben and get started."

Amy grinned across the table at her. Joni seemed to feel at home already – and Amy had the feeling they were going to get on famously.

The next morning, Joni was as good as her word – ready bright and early to get on with the work. When Amy started her daily session with Molly, the new stable girl came to watch, curious to know how the mare was progressing.

"She's been doing really well through muddy patches, areas of straw, stuff like that," explained Amy, leading Molly out of her stall. "She's so much more trusting than she was. But she's still got to deal with her fear of putting her feet in water. That's the thing she's most jumpy about because that's how she got injured."

Joni nodded. "How are you going to tackle it?"

"I'm going to set the hosepipe going so that it makes a really shallow stream across the yard," said Amy. "I'll lead her through it first, and if she's OK with that, we can move on to riding her through it."

"Sounds good," said Joni. "I can set the hose going for you, if you like."

Molly's trust in Amy had continued to grow, and she only spooked a little as they approached the water. Amy allowed the mare to take her time. She bent down to sniff it, nosing it with her soft muzzle. Then, without further ado, she responded to Amy's gentle tug on her halter and walked through it.

"Bravo!" called Joni from beside the tap. "That was great."

Amy smiled. "I'll try tacking her up and riding her through it now," she said.

Joni held Molly while Amy fetched her tack, then helped her do up the buckles on the mare's bridle and reach for the girth underneath her belly.

"D'you need a leg up?"

"No, I'll be fine, thanks," responded Amy, swinging herself lightly into the saddle. "Come on, Molly. Let's see how brave you'll be for me."

If anything, having Amy on her back seemed to offer Molly more reassurance. Amy nudged her forward with a gentle squeeze of her calves, and she stepped through the water without a murmur.

"You know what else you could do?" said Joni. "You could try sluicing down her legs with the hose. She's probably had that done before, after muddy rides — but it'll all help her get used to being in water again."

"Great idea," said Amy.

She dismounted and Joni turned the hose on Molly's feet. As she did so, it slipped, spraying Amy with water.

"Hey!" yelled Amy, laughing. "It's not my feet that need hosing."

"Sorry, Amy," giggled Joni. "Didn't mean it. Honest."

Molly flickered her ears at the sound of the girls laughing, and seemed unperturbed by the water shooting over her hooves. Joni hosed her hind legs too, just to make sure that she was truly unconcerned.

"A good morning's work," said Amy, as they led Molly back to her stall. "I just wish I didn't have to go to school. I'll have to hand you over to Ben and Ty now."

Later that evening, when Ben had taken Joni home, Amy and Ty sat in the tack room discussing how her first full day had gone.

"Absolutely no problems," Ty said. "Joni's great. She really pitched in with all the yard work. At one point there was nothing much for her to do, so she just sat and cleaned a whole load of tack without being asked."

"That's great," said Amy, looking around at the gleaming racks of tack. "It's just a shame that Ben has to go."

"Yes," agreed Ty. "He's arranged with his aunt to take Red away on Saturday afternoon. That'll be his last working day, too."

The finality of it suddenly hit Amy again. "I still somehow feel as though I failed with Ben," she said, her voice trembling. "You know, that he isn't more committed to Heartland methods?"

Ty shook his head. "You mustn't blame yourself," he said gently. "Ben's heart doesn't belong here. That doesn't mean he hasn't gained something from us. Think of all the horses and owners who come and go. Heartland gives them something that they can't find anywhere else and then they leave again. Maybe that's true for Ben."

Amy reflected on Ty's words, and realized they were true. Ben had given so much while he had been with them – but he had received a lot, too. Heartland had helped him to come to terms with his family, and it had brought him closer to Red. Now they were on the verge of real success, and that was all thanks to Heartland.

She lapsed into silence, resting her head on Ty's shoulder. "It's just all happened so quickly," she said. "We're not even going to have time to give him a proper send-off. It's too late to organize something for tomorrow night. I heard him say he's going out."

"I don't think he expects anything," said Ty. "But I guess it would have been nice."

"Maybe we can do something for him later," Amy thought out loud. "I'll talk to Lou. We can't just let him go like that."

"No," agreed Ty. He kissed the top of her head. "But no one else would have thought of it. I'm so lucky to be with you. Did you know that?"

Amy smiled up at him and shook her head. "I think I'm the lucky one," she said.

Red seemed to know it was a momentous occasion as Ben led him towards the trailer. He looked magnificent in his travelling rug, every inch a future champion, with his ears pricked forward and his nostrils flaring. He clattered up the ramp without any fuss.

"Have you got everything?" asked Amy. "I've had a quick look around the tack room but I couldn't see anything else of Red's."

Ben grinned. "I don't think I'd need to worry, anyway," he said. "Something tells me I'll be coming back here plenty!"

"You'd better," said Amy. She hadn't expected to feel quite so upset, but she couldn't hold back the tears. She ran forward to give Ben a big hug, remembering everything they had been through together – the flu, the tornado, Ty's coma… He was so much a part of the Heartland family.

"Thanks for everything, Amy," whispered Ben, and she heard a catch in his voice. She drew back, unable to speak.

Ben shook hands with Jack, and hugged both Ty and Lou. Then they all gathered around the cab as he clambered into the driving seat. He started the engine and the trailer roared into life.

"Take care!" called Ben, with a wave.

"Bye, Ben!" everyone chorused. "Good luck! See you soon!"

When the trailer had turned on to the road and disappeared, Amy looked around for Joni. She had kept a respectful distance while everyone had said their goodbyes, and Amy found her grooming Sugarfoot in the back barn.

"Goodbyes are awful, aren't they?" said Joni sympathetically. "I had a hard time saying goodbye to my mom and dad. Mom was really upset, like she'd just lost her baby or something."

Amy nodded silently, still not trusting herself to speak. Joni handed her the hoofpick, and Amy felt grateful to her for understanding that she didn't want to talk about it. She bent down to pick the little pony's feet, hiding her face until she'd recovered.

"I was wondering how things are going with Venture," said Joni after a while. "Ty was telling me a bit about him yesterday."

Amy put down the last hoof and straightened up, beginning to feel a bit better. "Not as well as I'd like, actually. Do you want to go up to his stall?" she suggested. "We're treating him with all the herbs and flower remedies we can, but they're not having much effect."

As they walked back up to the front yard, Amy explained more about the trauma that Venture had suffered, and how it was difficult to tell exactly where he was in pain.

"He's so depressed," she said. "But nothing seems to lift his spirits or bring him any comfort. We can't do active things like join-up because he's so unhappy moving around. And we keep getting phone calls from journalists to ask how he is, which makes it seem worse."

They reached Venture's stall and slipped inside. Amy told Joni which remedies they were using – Star of Bethlehem and Rock Rose flower remedies, and lavender oil for massages. Joni listened intently, then ran her fingers lightly over the horse, gauging his reaction to pressure in different places.

"I wish my mom could see him," she said. "I'll ask her about him the next time I talk to her. She's fantastic with horses like this."

"She's a vet, right?" asked Amy curiously.

"Yeah. But she's qualified in all sorts of other things, too. And she's really into the Bach remedies, like I told you."

"Sounds a lot like my mom," said Amy, with a little smile.

Joni looked at her questioningly, but didn't enquire. Amy was glad. She didn't feel like explaining everything right then. Her emotions were still running high from saying goodbye to Ben, and it was good to know that Joni knew where to draw the line. But it reminded her that she wanted to tell Marion about Ben leaving. There were still times when only her mom's ear would do.

"Do you think we could go to the cemetery tomorrow, Lou?" Amy asked later. "I'd really like to go soon. Sunday's not too busy for you, is it?"

The two sisters were washing up after dinner. Lou put a stack of plates into the cupboard and nodded. "That should be OK. I'm planning to see Scott after brunch for a couple of hours, but we could go after that."

"I'd like to get some flowers," said Amy. "I guess that means a detour."

"No problem," said Lou. "I'll get some, too."

Having explained to Ty where they were going, Lou and Amy

drove off the next day in the mid-afternoon. The weather was mild, and Amy felt for the first time that spring was in the air. She bought a hand-tied bunch of spring flowers to put on Marion's grave, while Lou chose some delicate yellow roses.

As they neared the cemetery, they both became quiet, lost in their own thoughts. They left the car and made their way to the familiar gravestone.

"Do you want to go first?" asked Amy. She guessed that her sister would want to spend some time at the grave alone, given that she had so much on her mind.

"OK. Thanks," said Lou, stepping forward to prop her flowers against the cold stone.

Amy wandered off while Lou stood alone at Marion's grave. Amy could hear her talking, but not what she said. She waited for a while, casting sidelong glances to check when Lou had finished, then slowly walked back. Lou gave her a quick, tremulous smile, and Amy saw that her eyes were wet. As she stepped forward and placed her bunch of flowers next to Lou's, she felt her own tears welling up, too.

"Hi, Mom," she said softly. "I've got so much to tell you. Ben's just left and it's made me miss you more than ever. I tried to make him stay, but I guess he needs to move on. There's a new stable hand called Joni and she talks about her mom a lot."

Amy paused as her tears began to fall. Then she brushed them away again with her sleeve and carried on. "I think you'd like her, Mom. She's great with the horses and already knows a lot of the remedies we use. She's a lot of fun, too. But it was really sad to see Ben go. He's decided to concentrate on competing. I guess he's like you and Dad were when you were young."

Amy stopped to think about her father, Tim Fleming, who had been an international showjumper until a terrible accident ended his competition career. It was only after separating from him that her mother had set up Heartland – until then, she had been part of the competition world, too.

"I keep learning, Mom," Amy carried on. "Ben leaving has taught me to accept that people have to move on from Heartland, not just the horses. I just wish you were here to teach me, too."

She stayed at the graveside for a few minutes longer. Lou joined her, and they silently clasped hands. Then, as if knowing instinctively when the other was ready to go, they both turned to leave.

They made their way back towards the parking lot, each lost in her own thoughts. Suddenly, a movement caught Amy's eye.

"Lou! Look," she said in a low voice, pointing across to the other side of the graveyard. There was a figure standing alone in front of one of the graves.

"It's Nancy," murmured Lou. "I wonder what she's doing here?"

The older woman hadn't seen them. Nancy stood for some time with her head bowed, then turned and walked slowly back to her car. Amy and Lou watched her get in and drive away.

"Her husband must be buried here," said Amy. Jack had told them that Nancy had been widowed several years before.

Lou nodded. "Shall we go and see at the gravestone?"

The two sisters followed the gravel paths around to the spot where Nancy had been standing. A fresh bouquet of scarlet tulips lay next to a pristine marble headstone.

"'My dearly beloved husband, Edward Marshall'..." Lou read aloud. "She's been a widow for almost ten years."

Amy felt slightly awkward, as though they were somehow trespassing on Nancy's private life. She stepped back. As she did so, she noticed that there was an identical bouquet of tulips on the next grave along. She glanced at the headstone and her mouth went dry.

"Lou..." she whispered.

"What is it?"

Amy pointed, unable to speak. They read the headstone in silence.

"'In loving memory of Jennifer Marshall, born 2nd November 1968, died 27th February 1983. Our precious Jen, taken too soon.'"

Lou and Amy stared at each other.

"Do you think...?" Amy began.

Lou's eyes filled with tears. "She had a daughter," she said, her voice breaking. "Nancy must have had a daughter."

Chapter Ten

Lou and Amy drove back to Heartland in shock. They found Jack in the living room reading the newspaper, and sat down on the sofa next to him.

"Grandpa," said Lou slowly. "Did you know that Nancy had a daughter?"

Jack looked up sharply. "Pardon?"

"Amy and I were just at the cemetery," Lou explained. "We saw Nancy there. She'd left flowers on the grave of someone called Jennifer Marshall, who died when she was fifteen."

Now it was Grandpa's turn to look shocked. Amy suddenly realized what it might mean to him, and her heart beat faster. He, too, had lost his daughter – but why wouldn't Nancy have told him about her own? After all, she knew about Marion.

"It might not have been her daughter," Amy said uncertainly, half wishing it not to be true.

"It must have been," Lou insisted. "Why else would she be buried next to Nancy's husband?"

Grandpa still looked stunned. "I've seen pictures in her house," he said at last. "A fair-haired girl. Looks a tiny bit like you, Lou. But I always assumed it was her sister's daughter..."

"I guess it explains a lot," said Amy, thinking of the night that

Nancy had left. *I have a very good idea of what that room might mean to you*, she'd said. And getting involved with Lou's wedding plans... It all made sense now.

Grandpa nodded, looking at Lou. "Well..." he began.

Lou's gaze dropped to the floor.

"I think we should go and visit Nancy," Amy said quietly.

"Yes," whispered Lou. "I need to apologize to her. She ... she must understand grief like we do."

"Hey, Amy!" Joni called cheerily as Amy trudged into the yard in her school clothes. "Good day at school?"

Amy pulled a face. "The usual. I'll just go and change. I'll be with you in a minute."

Amy threw on her yard clothes, her spirits lifting. She hated being at school instead of being around to work with Ty and help Joni settle in, but at least it was fun when she got back. She hurried down to the yard and found Joni leaning over Venture's half-door.

"Any improvement?" asked Amy, coming up behind her.

Joni shook her head. "I've had an idea, though," she said. She hesitated. "I don't want to interfere or anything, but I've been talking to my mom, and she asked if you'd thought of trying acupuncture."

"Acupuncture?" Amy frowned. "I don't know much about it, to be honest."

"My mom's a practitioner," Joni went on. "It's one of the things she trained in after getting her vet certificate. We use it a lot on our mares. It's great for dealing with physical pain, but

110

it's also a holistic treatment. You can use it to get to the bottom of physical and emotional pain at the same time."

Amy was interested at once. "Don't you have to use needles for it?"

"Yes, but it doesn't really hurt, not like having an injection. It's based on Chinese medicine," Joni explained. "It's all about the body having a constant flow of energy along lines called meridians. When you're unhealthy or injured, the channels can get blocked or unbalanced. Acupuncture works on unblocking the meridians with really fine needles, so that the energy can flow freely again and the body can heal itself."

"But how do you know which channels are blocked?"

"By assessing all the symptoms, basically," said Joni. "But it's more complex than that. You have to know all about anatomy. The channels have places called points, which is where you put the needles in."

"And it really works?" Amy was fascinated.

Joni shrugged and laughed. "Sure seems to. Scientists can't explain why, but it's been practised for thousands of years. My mom swears by it. I'm learning all the principles myself so that I can practise acupressure, which is a bit like acupuncture without the needles. You can do that without being a vet."

Amy was impressed – and Venture's treatment had been going so badly that it was good to hear about something that just might help. "Do you really think it might be the answer for Venture?"

Joni nodded. "I'll need to talk to my mom again first. She's coming down in a few days with a load of my stuff, so if she thinks it's the right thing, she could give him a treatment."

"That's brilliant!" exclaimed Amy. "I can't wait to tell Ty — let's go find him!"

They ran down to the training ring where Ty was lungeing a new arrival, Indigo. He reined the horse in when he saw them approaching the gate and walked over. He listened intently to what Joni had to say, then nodded.

"I've heard of acupuncture being good for horses," he said. "The problem is that we don't have a practitioner anywhere near here, as far as I know."

"That's what's so great," enthused Amy. "Joni's mom is coming down soon. She'll be able to treat Venture herself."

"Sounds perfect," said Ty. Then he frowned. "We need to make sure that Scott's happy with it, though. And Sergeant Garcia. They might have objections to it."

Joni looked slightly anxious. "My mom's a qualified vet," she said. "She works with lots of horses back home."

"Sure," said Ty gently. "But Scott is Venture's vet while he's at Heartland. We have to make sure he's happy with it."

Amy knew that Ty was right, but she felt sorry that their enthusiasm had been dampened, all the same. "I don't mind calling Scott," she offered, giving Joni a warm smile. "I'll call him after supper. And Sergeant Garcia, too."

To her surprise, Amy felt slightly nervous when it came to making the phone calls. She didn't know anything about acupuncture herself, and Joni was so new... It could be awkward if it didn't work out — especially if the press jumped on the idea, too.

She decided to phone Mark Garcia first. He sounded surprised to hear from her, but there was a warmth in his voice that she hadn't registered before. She explained that they wanted to try a new kind of treatment.

"Obviously we can't be sure what effect it will have exactly," she explained. "And we'd need your permission before we go ahead."

"It sounds like a good idea to me," said Mark. "Thank you, Amy. I have a lot of respect for your tenacity. It's a fine quality, you know."

"Oh!" Amy felt touched, and slightly embarrassed. "Well, like I said. I know all about hanging on in there."

"Yes. I've been thinking about what you told me," the police sergeant said. "And I think you're right. I don't think I could forgive myself if I didn't hold on."

"And is everyone else OK with that?" asked Amy anxiously. "Your superiors, I mean?"

Mark Garcia gave a sigh. "Well, it's been quite a week," he admitted. "There are obviously all sorts of prioritization issues in our department when it comes to funding. But I've thrashed things out. My bosses have agreed to continue Venture's treatment — as long as I partly fund it myself."

Amy gasped.

"So I've agreed to it. I have savings," he went on. "It's the least I can do." He paused. "I might easily have given up, you know. But you've helped me see beyond that. I'm with you — and Venture — whatever it takes."

"I'm so pleased," Amy said warmly. "I know it's the right decision. I really do."

She came off the phone, her optimism surging. As long as Scott agreed too, they might really be getting somewhere. Amy rang the vet with her heart thumping.

"Acupuncture?" mused Scott on the other end of the line. "Well…" He hesitated. "There's no guarantee it'll work, you know. As far as I'm aware, it's not widely used on horses yet."

"But do you think it might be worth trying?" Amy persisted. "I mean, would you allow us to try it on Venture? Joni's mom's a qualified vet."

"I wouldn't say no," said Scott cautiously. "If it's carried out properly, it couldn't do any harm. I'd just be careful about getting your hopes up too high, that's all."

Amy breathed a sigh of relief. They could go ahead, at least. "Thanks, Scott. I know what you're saying and I won't expect miracles. I'm just glad there's something else we can try. It might be Venture's last hope."

With all the excitement about Venture, it was difficult to concentrate at school the next day. Moreover, Amy had agreed with Lou that they would visit Nancy right after school. It was a slightly nerve-wracking prospect, and Amy knew she'd be glad when it was over with – though not half as glad as Lou would be.

"I hope she's in," said Lou as they drove down the road later that day. "I don't know if I'd have the courage to try this twice!"

"I know what you mean," said Amy.

"I just feel so bad," Lou went on. "You know, for what I said to her."

Amy gave her sister a sympathetic smile. She was glad she could be there for moral support. It wasn't often that Lou needed it, but the row was still hanging over the whole family. Amy knew that Grandpa had visited Nancy a few times since, but there had been no suggestion of her coming back to Heartland — mainly, Amy suspected, because it was up to Lou to make amends.

Nancy's house was painted a pale eggshell blue, the small front garden densely planted with rose bushes. Lou and Amy made their way up the path to the front door. Lou took a deep breath and rang the bell.

The house was very quiet, and it seemed for ever before they heard the sound of footsteps in the hallway. The door opened and Nancy stood there, holding gardening gloves in one hand. She stared at them for a moment, then quickly recovered and smiled.

"Why, this is a nice surprise!" she said. "Will you come in?"

Amy and Lou followed her through the house to the kitchen, which had a back door leading on to a porch overlooking the back garden.

"It's such a lovely day, I've been outside," said Nancy, keeping her smile bright as she filled the kettle and switched it on. She bustled around, bringing out a tray and a set of china teacups. "Would you like to sit out? It's really not too cold on the porch. I'll make some tea."

Amy stepped through on to the wooden deck, where there

were comfortable wicker chairs looking out through large windows on to the garden. Gardening was obviously one of Nancy's great loves; even though the spring flowers had only just started making an appearance, the garden was full of colour.

She and Lou were just sitting down on the chairs when Nancy came through.

"What kind of tea would you like? My favourite is Earl Grey. It was Edward's favourite too, you see. But I know it's not to everyone's taste – I haven't converted Jack yet!" She gave a little laugh.

"Do you have any peppermint tea?" Lou asked.

"Yes, I think so," said Nancy. "How about you, Amy?"

"I'll try the Earl Grey," said Amy. "Thanks."

Nancy disappeared again, leaving them to stare out on to the garden. Lou was restless, and stood up again to wander to the window. Amy joined her and they looked out over the well-kept lawn – very different from the tiny garden at Heartland, which had been rather neglected since Marion died.

"It's a beautiful garden," Amy commented when Nancy came back. "You must put a lot of work into it."

Nancy placed the tea tray on the coffee table. "Well, it keeps me busy," she said. "Keeps my mind off things." She handed a cup to Lou. "Here's your peppermint tea. I've made a pot for us, Amy."

They watched as Nancy laid out cups and saucers and poured the tea.

Lou took a deep breath. "I guess you know why we've come," she began. "I ... I need to say sorry."

Nancy passed a cup over to Amy and settled back into her chair. "Yes. I thought you might," she said quietly.

Lou took a sip of her tea, then placed it back in the saucer. "There's no excuse really. I... What I said..." She stopped. "I didn't expect to find it so hard, having someone else around at Heartland. Someone ... older."

"I understand," said Nancy. "No one can replace your mother." She looked down at the teacup in her hands. "It hasn't been easy for me either, spending time in a family again. It's brought back a lot of memories."

To Amy's dismay, Nancy's eyes filled with tears.

"We saw you in the graveyard on Sunday," Amy said softly. "We were there putting flowers on Mom's grave."

"And we guessed that Jennifer was your daughter," Lou put in.

Nancy nodded. The tears in her eyes spilled over, and she quickly pulled a handkerchief from her sleeve to dab them.

"I'm so sorry," said Lou. "I didn't know. None of us did."

"No. I know. It was silly of me," said Nancy, her voice trembling. "I just thought that you all had enough grief to deal with, without knowing about mine. I was wrong."

Amy felt her sadness for Marion welling up all over again. Would it ever begin to fade? Nancy was still grieving for her daughter many years after her death. Perhaps the pain never went away. Amy took a gulp of her tea and realized that her hand was shaking.

There was silence for a moment.

Lou put her teacup back on the table. "I guess, perhaps with me and Scott getting married, it must have been difficult..." She trailed off.

"Because it reminded me of Jennifer?" finished Nancy for her. "Perhaps. I'd always imagined her wedding day, that's for sure."

Amy saw the anguish in her eyes and understood. Just as Lou longed for Marion to be at her wedding, so Nancy must have hoped to see Jennifer married, with a long happy life in front of her.

Nancy blew her nose. "I'm so glad you both came. At least everything's out in the open now. It can't take away the pain, but it might ease it a little."

Lou nodded. "Thank you for being so understanding. I don't feel like I deserve it − but I'm really glad we came, too." She stood up. "We ought to get back. Grandpa's cooking supper for us. Can we help you clear away the tea things?"

"No, no, you get going," said Nancy. "I know how busy you both are."

She ushered them to the door, back to her usual bustling self.

"Thanks so much for everything, Nancy." Lou leaned forward to give the older woman a kiss on the cheek.

Amy stepped outside, then turned impulsively and gave Nancy a hug. "Come back to Heartland soon," she said. "I've missed you."

Nancy looked surprised and pleased. "Why, thank you, Amy," she said. "I'm sure I'll drop by before long." She turned to Lou, a mischievous look in her eyes. "And don't forget. I'm still happy to bake that cake − if you'll let me!"

Chapter Eleven

"That's it, show her you're feeling confident. Nice firm aids," called Amy, as Eloise nudged Molly forward through a mound of dead leaves that Amy had arranged in the training ring. "Don't give her a chance to feel you're doubting her."

Eloise sat deep in the saddle and drove Molly on, and to her obvious delight, the mare dropped her nose on to the bit and walked confidently through the leaves. Amy saw the excitement on Eloise's face and grinned. "This is the best part," she said to Joni, who was sitting on the fence beside her. "Seeing a horse change, and knowing she's almost ready to go back to her owner."

Joni nodded. "I can see that," she said. "They look so good together."

Amy left Joni at the gate and jogged over to Eloise and Molly in the centre of the training ring. "Now for the big test," Amy said to Eloise. "I want you to ride her through water. We've given her lots of preparation so she should be fine. The key is going to be your confidence, not hers. Do you think you're ready for that?"

Eloise looked nervous, then smiled. "You've done a fantastic job with her, Amy," she said. "Do you really think she'll be OK?"

"Yes, I do," said Amy. "She's been happy going through water for about a week now. I can ride her through it without any problems. So there's no reason why you shouldn't."

She led the way out of the training ring and up on to the track that led to Clairdale Ridge. Joni joined her and they walked alongside Molly, chatting to Eloise.

"There's a little stream that runs across the track up here," Amy explained. "You can try riding her through that. Just remember – all you have to do is believe in her."

"OK," said Eloise. "She's going so well, I think I do believe in her, you know."

Amy looked at the mare, who was walking along with her ears pricked and her neck arched. Curious as ever, she was clearly delighted to be out on the trails, but she wasn't pulling or napping. She was listening to her rider and responding willingly to her commands.

"There you go," said Amy, stopping and pointing along the track. "The stream's just ahead. You go through it. We'll stay here and watch so we don't get in the way."

Eloise took a deep breath and nudged Molly on. The horse continued up the track, then stopped when she spotted the stream. It wasn't particularly deep, but it was quite fast-flowing, gurgling over pebbles and glinting in the light that filtered through the trees.

"Come on, Molly," said Eloise firmly. "We're going through it."

She gave her a determined squeeze with her calves, and Molly stepped forward tentatively, placing one hoof in the stream. Amy saw the mare stiffen as her foot disappeared into the water. But Eloise kept up the pressure. Molly took another step, then another, until she had walked right through it. On the other side, Eloise turned in the saddle and gave a whoop of triumph.

"We did it!" she called back. "I can't believe it!"

Amy and Joni laughed. "Bring her back again then!" Amy called.

This time, Molly didn't even hesitate. She splashed through the stream, and Eloise broke into a trot as she rejoined the others. Happily, they set off back down the track to Heartland.

"Do you think I can take her home soon?" Eloise asked as they entered the yard.

Amy nodded. "As soon as you like," she said with a smile.

Lou was humming a tune when Amy went inside for supper. Her whole mood seemed to have lifted since their visit to Nancy a couple of days earlier. Grandpa was clearly delighted that she had plucked up the courage to apologize, and to Amy's relief, the family atmosphere was very much back to normal.

"Eloise is coming to collect Molly on Sunday," Amy told her. "We have quite a few spaces now – Dazzle and Red have gone, Molly's stall will be free on Sunday..."

"OK, I'll have a look at the waiting list," said Lou. "Leave it with me."

"There's something else, too," said Amy. "I feel really bad that we didn't give Ben any kind of farewell party. Do you think we could do something for him soon?"

Lou looked dismayed. "Amy! Why didn't you mention it

before? Of course. When were you thinking of?"

"Well, it might be better to wait until Mrs Janssen's visit is over," said Amy. "She's arriving tomorrow to do the first of Venture's acupuncture treatments. Maybe next Saturday?"

Lou grabbed her diary and checked the dates. "That should be fine," she said. "Do you want to ask him if that's OK?"

Amy nodded. "I'll ask him when he brings Joni over tomorrow," she replied.

The next morning, Amy made sure she was in the yard when Ben and Joni arrived. She waved to Ben to stop him from driving off again. It was odd to see him turn around ready to drive away – it still felt as though he should be getting out to crack on with the chores.

"Ben! Can I have a word?" she called.

Ben got out of his car. "Sure."

"We were wondering if you'd come over to dinner one night," said Amy. "We never got to give you a proper send-off. I hope it isn't too late!"

"Hey! That'd be great," said Ben. "I wasn't expecting anything ... but you know, I'm really missing you guys." He looked around the yard and let his gaze rest on Joni, who was just visible, already mucking out the stalls.

Amy smiled. "Yeah. We miss you too. It's not the same without you around."

Ben gave a little shrug. His eyes were still on Joni's back, bent over her fork. "It's nice of you to say so, Amy," he said. "But I can see that Joni really fits in, more than I ever did. I guess in a way, she was what you needed all the time."

Amy's eyes flew wide. "Ben! That's not how it was at all. You were brilliant. You did so much. I don't know what we would have done without you, especially when ... when everything went wrong. In fact," she found herself blurting out, "I felt as if it was my fault that you decided to leave. Maybe if you'd had more of a chance to join in with the treatments—"

"No, no, no," Ben interrupted her. "Don't think that. Please." He shook his head vehemently, then ran a hand through his hair. "You did everything you could to get me involved," he said. "It was me who didn't want to. Not fully. I learned loads, but I could never take my attention away from Red for long enough to really engage with it."

"Do you really feel that?" Amy asked slowly.

"Yes," Ben reassured her. "I do."

They looked at each other, and Amy thought of what Ty had said. *Ben's heart doesn't belong here.* It was good to hear it from his own lips, however hard it was to understand. But now, seeing him leaning on the door of his pick-up, she was beginning to accept it at last. Impulsively, she reached out and hugged him.

"We were thinking of next Saturday for your do," she said when she pulled away again. "Will that be OK?"

Ben frowned. "Could be tricky. I'm competing that day," he said. He thought for a minute, then his face cleared. "It's an early class, though. How about you and Joni watch me jump? Then we can all come back here together afterwards."

Amy nodded enthusiastically. "Hey, I haven't been to a show for ages! That would be really fun. Let's do it!"

Amy stood waving as Ben drove off, feeling much happier. It was good to have cleared the air with him. As his pick-up disappeared in a cloud of dust, she started thinking about the day ahead. *Venture's first acupuncture session*, she thought, and felt a thrill of excitement. It was going to be fascinating, seeing a new way of treating the horses.

She helped Joni finish off the mucking out, and was just emptying the wheelbarrow when she heard the familiar sound of Scott's jeep coming up the driveway. She remembered that he had decided to come and watch the first acupuncture session.

"Hi Amy," Scott called, slamming the jeep door. "I know I'm a bit early but I thought I'd drop in and see Lou. How's the patient?"

Amy shook her head. "Not much change," she said. "I'm really hoping that the acupuncture makes a difference." She gazed questioningly at Scott. "I know you don't think there's much chance…"

Scott looked serious. "Well, I didn't mean it quite like that. I think it depends a lot on the particular problem, and the particular horse," he said. "But like any other treatment, it's not guaranteed to work. We just have to hope for the best."

Amy nodded, and spotted Joni looking on with an anxious expression. She went over. "Will your mom be here soon?" Amy asked. "Your uncle's bringing her over from Baltimore, isn't he?"

"She should be here anytime soon," Joni replied, taking a deep breath. "Say, Amy, if it's not right for Venture, sometimes it's not the right thing, you know."

"I'll understand," Amy reassured her. "Venture's had every treatment under the sun. It'll be amazing if this works for him. If it doesn't, we'll just have to find something else."

Joni looked relieved. "Well, we'll just have to see what Mom decides," she said. "Fingers crossed she thinks it's right for him!"

They both turned at the sound of another car coming up the driveway. "That's my uncle's car," said Joni.

A silver Chrysler pulled into the front yard. Joni ran forward to the passenger side and Mrs Janssen climbed out. Amy watched as she gave Joni a big hug. She was struck by how much Greta looked like Joni; but she was taller, and her straight blonde hair was shorter, cropped close to her head. The man who got out of the driver's seat could only be Greta's brother, a few years older perhaps, but with the same blond hair and smiling eyes.

"You must be Amy," said Mrs Janssen. "I've heard so much about you." She held out her hand. "Greta Janssen — and this is my brother, Leif."

Amy smiled and shook hands. Lou and Scott came out of the farmhouse and Ty appeared from the feed room, so Amy did a round of introductions. Once they were over, Leif climbed back into his car, saying he'd be back in a couple of hours, and drove off with a cheery wave.

"Would you like a coffee before you meet Venture?" Amy asked Greta.

"Oh, I had one not long ago," smiled Greta. "I'm keen to see your patient more than anything, and get started. But a coffee when I've finished would be just great!"

"I'll leave you to it," said Ty. "We don't want Venture to be swamped with visitors." He reached out to touch Amy's hand, before heading off to the feed room. "Good luck," he added.

Amy led Scott, Joni and Greta across the front yard. Greta stopped at each stable door to greet the horses. Joni had obviously told her all about them. Amy felt a pang as she realized how much Marion and Greta would have had in common, and how much they would have liked each other. They reached Venture's stall and Amy slid back the bolt. As usual, the police horse was standing at the back. He rolled the whites of his eyes nervously at the group of people entering his stall. Amy went to his head to try and reassure him.

"I think I'll watch from outside," said Joni. "It's a bit crowded in here."

She slipped out again to lean over the half-door instead. As Greta began to study the horse, Amy quickly ran through his history, explaining how it was impossible to tell the extent of his physical pain because he seemed so depressed.

Greta nodded. "So, non-specific pain, probably in the back region, combined with the effects of trauma." She turned to Scott. "Is there anything else you can tell me?"

Scott shook his head. "No. He's had thorough spinal checks and extensive medical treatment for weeks. There doesn't seem to be anything else physical that I can help you with."

Greta stepped forward and placed her hand lightly on the police horse's back. He shifted uneasily, his ears flattened. Greta began to press with one finger more firmly in particular places, and watched Venture's reaction. Sometimes he seemed more sensitive, at other times less so.

"At the moment, I'm just assessing which meridians need unblocking," she explained to Scott and Amy. "I would say from his reactions so far that acupuncture could definitely offer him a way forward. There's one particular set of points that seems to be provoking a response in him. Are you happy for me to go ahead?"

"Yes, please," said Amy. "It won't hurt him, will it?"

Greta smiled. "No. The most he'll feel is a dull tingling when I put the needles in. That's all humans ever feel. Once they're in, you might be surprised at how much he relaxes."

"How long do you keep them in?" asked Scott as Greta opened her case and selected one of the fine, sterile needles.

"It varies from horse to horse," said Greta. "In Venture's case, I'll probably leave them there for twenty minutes or so. Perhaps slightly longer."

Expertly, she began to insert a series of needles into different points on Venture's neck and back. Amy counted nine altogether. She watched, fascinated, as Greta stepped back for a moment, then gently manipulated the needles one at a time. She threw a quick glance at Joni, who was leaning over the half-door looking a lot less anxious.

After a few moments, Amy realized that Venture's eyes had begun to close.

"Venture's falling asleep!"

Greta nodded. "That often happens. He'll probably remain drowsy for a while afterwards."

Amy stroked Venture's nose in wonderment. She hadn't seen him looking this relaxed ever. She grinned at Joni and the stable girl grinned back, her blue eyes sparkling.

After about twenty-five minutes, Greta quietly removed the needles and packed them away. She stroked Venture's neck for a moment. "Well, that's it," she said. "All done for now. I'm going to be around for a few days, so I can come back on Monday and then Wednesday, if that's convenient for you. Three treatments should help him a lot. After that, Joni can continue with acupressure on the same points — as long as she follows my instructions closely, it will have almost as much benefit as the needles."

Joni's face lit up. "Is that OK, Amy?" she asked. "I've got my preliminary qualification. I'll make sure that Mom talks me through the meridians she's stimulating."

"Acupressure just uses finger pressure, doesn't it?" Amy checked. She glanced at Scott. "That should be fine, shouldn't it?"

Scott nodded. "I'm happy with that," he said. "I have to say, I'm very impressed with it all. It makes me wonder about training myself."

They all stepped out of the stall, leaving Venture with his eyes half-shut and his lower lip drooping, a sure sign that he had drifted off happily. Amy stayed to take one last look at him as the others made their way to the farmhouse to tell Lou the good news.

"You're going to get better, Venture," she whispered. "It's been a long journey, but it looks like we've found the right treatment for you at last."

Chapter Twelve

Lou placed a fresh plateful of muffins on the table, then sat down again. "I've asked Nancy to come to Ben's celebration next Saturday," she said casually. "And she said yes."

Jack and Amy stopped eating and looked at her in surprise. Jack's face broke into a smile. "That was nice of you, Lou," he said. "I'm sure she'd love to come."

Amy caught her sister's eye and grinned.

"She said she wasn't sure about coming, at first." Lou looked down at her slice of toast, going slightly pink. "But I told her she's part of the family now."

No one said anything, but Grandpa reached out and squeezed Lou's hand. Amy felt glad, and also realized that Lou's words were true: Nancy was part of the family. She could never replace Marion, but she brought a new warmth and energy to the house; and she was clearly very important to Grandpa. Amy quickly threw a smile at Ty, who was sitting quietly next to her, not getting involved.

Amy touched his hand. "You're part of the family, too, you know," she whispered.

"Thank you," Ty whispered back.

It was Sunday morning. Joni had taken the day off to visit her mother in Baltimore, so it was just the four of them sitting at the brunch table. When they had finished eating, Ty and Amy did the dishes together, then headed out into the yard.

"Venture's definitely looking brighter today," commented Ty as they approached his stall. "But I guess there's still a long way to go before we could even think about saddling him again."

Venture looked around with his ears pricked as they peered into his stall. It was true: the lines of his body did seem more relaxed, and his expression was curious for once.

"I'll take him for a gentle walk down to the paddocks today," said Ty. "It's a nice day. He could stay out for a bit. What time is Eloise coming for Molly?"

"Anytime now," said Amy. "I'll miss her. She's a star."

She fetched a broom and began to sweep the front yard. Within a few minutes, Molly had left her haynet and was watching Amy over her half-door, her intelligent eyes following her every movement.

"Hey there, Molly," laughed Amy, stopping to scratch her neck. "It's almost home time for you. Did you know that?"

As Molly snorted and blew over her hair, Amy heard the sound of a jeep and trailer rattling up the drive. "In fact," she said to the horse, "it might be sooner rather than later. I think this is Eloise now."

Sure enough, it was Eloise who jumped out of the driver's seat, grinning. She walked over to Amy and reached up to give Molly a stroke on the nose.

"Hi, Eloise," said Amy. "She's all yours again. I'll go and grab her tack."

"Thanks, Amy," responded Eloise. "I can hardly believe she's actually coming home."

Amy jogged over to the tack room and picked out Molly's tack and accessories. With the bridle slung over her shoulder and the saddle hoisted on to her arm, she marched back out again. Then she stopped. Eloise had led Molly out of her stall and was giving the mare a big hug around the neck.

Amy smiled. Through join-up, she had built a strong bond of trust with the mare – but there was no doubt who Molly loved most of all.

"I think Sergeant Garcia will be showing up soon," said Amy, as Greta Janssen laid out her case of needles once more. It was Wednesday, and Greta had arrived to do the third acupuncture session. "He was really keen to see one of the sessions, or part of it at least. I suggested he came to this one, if that's OK with you?"

"Fine," said Greta. "I hope he's not expecting miracles, though. It's going to take this fellow a long time to get back to full form."

Amy smiled. "I think any change at all will seem like a miracle to Sergeant Garcia," she said. "And he's totally committed for waiting for as long as it takes."

Venture was looking a lot more lively and more attentive to what was going on around him. In the last five days the sense of stiffness and pain in his body had begun to ease quite visibly. When Greta had arrived, he had actually whickered a welcome, as though he knew she could bring him some comfort.

"I've shown Joni exactly what I'm doing so that she'll be

able to continue with acupressure after I've gone," said Greta, as she began the careful process of inserting the needles. Joni watched closely. "Acupressure is very effective and relaxing."

"I tried T-touch, but he hated it," said Amy, puzzled. "You do that with pressure from your fingers, too. Why should acupressure be different?"

"T-touch isn't based on the meridians and points," Greta explained. "It's relaxing, but it's not working with the body's channels of energy in the same way. Acupressure doesn't work along the surface of the skin — it's triggering the points underneath it."

Amy looked up as a shadow fell across the door. It was Sergeant Garcia. He looked astonished to see the arrangement of needles sticking out of Venture, but stood quietly outside, his eyes wide, as Greta manipulated each one in turn. By the time she took them out again, Venture had started to doze off again.

As Greta packed away her needles, Amy invited the sergeant to come inside the stall.

"Greta, this is Sergeant Garcia, Venture's rider," she said.

Greta shook his hand and smiled. "Venture's a fine horse," she told him warmly. "I think he may be on the mend now."

The sergeant stroked Venture's neck. "He's already changed in just a few days," he said. "Thank you. I can't tell you how much this means to me."

His face broke into a smile, and Amy handed him Venture's

lead rope. "He's quite sleepy at the moment," she said. "But maybe you'd like to walk down to the paddocks with him later?"

"I might do that," said Mark. "Thanks."

Amy took Joni and Greta to the farmhouse, where Lou had some coffee brewing. Joni was looking a little sad, as this was her mother's last evening before going back to Canada.

"Would you like to stay for supper?" Lou offered. "There's plenty of food."

"That's very kind, but no, thank you," said Greta. "I have an early morning flight, so I need to get back to Baltimore."

"Well, it's been great meeting you," said Lou. "I'm sure we'll see you again, now that Joni's working here."

"Of course. And I'll be expecting Joni to give me detailed updates on Venture's progress," Greta replied, putting down her coffee cup. "I must be going." She shrugged on her coat. "Goodbye. And see you soon."

Amy accompanied Greta and Joni outside, then left them to say goodbye to each other. She wondered how Sergeant Garcia and Venture were doing, so she wandered over to his stall. It was empty, so she walked down the track towards the paddocks.

In the early evening light, the sergeant was leading the horse along one side of the top paddock, one hand on the dark brown neck for reassurance. Venture was striding out calmly, his neck arched and his ears pricked forward.

Amy held back, not wanting to disturb them. She watched for a moment longer then slipped away, her heart full of hope.

Through all the changes that had taken place – Ben leaving, Joni arriving – Heartland had found a solution for Venture's problem. He had a long road before him, but at least he had made the first step.

"Ben won the blue ribbon!" Amy called out cheerily, opening the kitchen door. She was greeted by a blast of heat, a big contrast with the cold air outside. It was Saturday. Lou and Nancy were bustling around with their cheeks flushed, the preparations for the evening's dinner well under way. Nancy was rinsing a big pile of blueberries, while Lou was stirring something on the stove.

"Hey, that's great!" exclaimed Lou. "So it's a double celebration!"

"He's up in the clouds," laughed Amy, going over to peer into Lou's saucepan. It was full of a rich chilli sauce that smelt wonderful. "What can I do to help?"

Nancy and Lou both called out answers at once.

"You can grate some cheese for the tortillas," said Lou.

"You can roll out some pastry for my pie," Nancy suggested.

Amy looked from one to the other and laughed. "Are you going to fight over me?"

Lou grinned. "I think you should do Nancy's pastry," she said. "The cheese can wait until the last minute."

Feeling unexpectedly happy, Amy set to with the rolling pin. Things were certainly different when Nancy was around, and it was a relief that she and Lou were getting on again. Lost in her reflections, Amy failed to notice that her strip of pastry was turning out far too long and thin, and would never fit into a pie tin.

"Hmmm," said Nancy good-humouredly, when she saw the pastry. "I can see that cooking isn't your strong point. Maybe we should banish you to the stables. What d'you think, Lou?"

Lou laughed. "Nothing would make Amy happier," she teased.

There was barely enough room for everyone when they sat down to eat — and certainly not enough room for all the food. Lou had made a Mexican feast of nachos and soft tortillas to fill with the delicious chilli sauce, and lots of toppings.

"My favourite," declared Ben, sitting down next to Joni.

Amy squeezed herself on to the kitchen bench between Ty and Grandpa and looked around happily. Joni was chatting with Ben about the show that day while Scott, who had just arrived, was washing his hands at the sink. Lou was hurriedly putting serving spoons in all the bowls.

Ty began filling up Amy's plate for her. "Guacamole?" he asked, hovering a spoonful over her plate.

Amy nodded. "Please. And lots of sour cream and grated cheese."

It was all delicious. Amy took a handful of crunchy nachos and passed the bowl to Grandpa and Nancy, who was just sitting down next to him.

"Now don't let me forget that pie," said Nancy. "It needs to stay in the oven for another fifteen minutes. Any more and

Amy's pastry will be burned." She smiled at Amy and gave her a wink.

Amy laughed. "It's good to have you back, Nancy," she said.

"Why, thank you, Amy," replied Nancy. "It's good to be back. And it's great to know we can get everything out in the open. I think you and Lou have a lot of courage. You must be proud of them, Jack."

Jack nodded. "Sure am," he said, giving Amy a grin.

Amy spooned some sour cream over her tortilla and picked it up with her fingers to take a bite. Nancy's words had warmed her to the core and she was so glad that Grandpa had found someone special after all this time ... and however hard it might be, it was good to realize how much they had in common, too.

The feast was soon demolished, and Nancy began to get the next stage under way. Just as she placed her magnificent blueberry pie on the table, Lou cleared her throat to catch everyone's attention. Amy saw her exchange a meaningful glance with Scott. What was going on?

"Before we have dessert, Scott and I would like to say something," said Lou. Everyone went quiet and listened expectantly.

"First of all, congratulations to Ben for winning today," Lou carried on. "And good luck for the future. I hope you'll come back —" She stopped speaking as everyone applauded.

Ben grinned happily and raised his glass. "Thank you, everybody."

"And I especially hope you'll come back on our wedding

day," finished Lou, with a broad smile. "Scott and I have made a decision. We're going to get married in the fall."

There was a thunder of noise as everyone banged their spoons on the table and cheered.

Then Scott got to his feet, looking nervous. "There's just one more thing," he said. He turned to face Jack. "We'd like to use this happy occasion to ask your permission to be married at Heartland."

Jack looked stunned, then a huge smile spread across his face. He got up and gave Lou and Scott each a hug. Amy sneaked a look at Nancy and caught her wiping away a tear.

"Nothing would give me more pleasure," said Grandpa. With a quick glance at Nancy, he added, "I'm so proud of both Lou and Amy. I'm lucky to have two wonderful granddaughters. And to see one of you getting happily married is the most wonderful thing I could ever hope for." He cleared his throat and reached for his glass. "To Lou and Scott."

"To Lou and Scott!" everyone chorused.

"And to happy futures," added Jack. "For those leaving and those arriving. We wish you all the very best, Ben. And we hope that Joni will be happy here with us at Heartland. Happy futures!"

"Happy futures!" rang out around the table.

Later, as they waved Ben and Joni goodbye in the yard, Amy went over to Ty and leaned against him. He smiled and put his arm around her.

"So much change," Amy murmured. "But I'm glad you're still here."

"I'll always be here for you, Amy," said Ty. "I'm not going anywhere."

Amy sighed. "You were right about Ben," she said. "Heartland isn't right for everyone, not for ever. People have to move on as well as horses."

Ty pulled her closer to him. "People move on, and people arrive," he said. "Would you ever have imagined that Joni would be so great?"

Amy shook her head and laughed. She looked across the yard and saw Nancy chatting happily with Lou and Scott. The Heartland family kept shifting and moving on ... but however much it changed, there was always something worth holding on to, something to hold fast.